I0728075

# UNDER FALLING SKIES

## THE TRAVELS OF SCOUT SHANNON

### KATE MACLEOD

Copyright © 2017 by Kate MacLeod

All rights reserved.

No part of this book may be reproduced in any form or by any electronic or mechanical means, including information storage and retrieval systems, without written permission from the author, except for the use of brief quotations in a book review.

Cover image by Benjamin P. Roque

Ratatoskr Press logo by Aidan Vincent Kise

ISBN 978-1-946552-51-8

❦ Created with Vellum

1

THE SUN CLIMBED EVER HIGHER in the sky, its bulbous red mass condensing to a tighter, whiter heat as it ascended. Scout could feel it behind her, pounding on her back as she leaned over the handlebars of her bike. The air was still night-cool and filled with the smells of the tiny flowers that bloomed on the vines that strangled the tumble of boulders around her, their probing tendrils digging ever deeper into the splits in the rock faces. But the flowers were closing against the coming day and the coolness of the air did little against the heat Scout was creating pedaling her bike up the steep hillside path. Now that the nighttime insects had ceased their buzzing choruses, the only sound was her own labored breathing and the occasional skitter of loose rock cascading back down the hillside behind her.

She was drenched with sweat, could see it falling in drops to briefly make clean streaks in the red dust clinging to her handlebars and coating the tanned skin of her hands and forearms. She ignored it all—the drops of sweat, the rising sun, the building sticky dryness in her mouth—and focused only on pushing one pedal down, then the other. It was a lurching sort of progress up the last bit of hill, the slowness combined with the weight of her saddlebags challenging her balance even as the tires slipped over the layers of dry, dusty clay.

It would be easier to get off and walk the bike the rest of the way up, but she never did. That would be giving up. And Scout never gave up.

At last, she reached the top of the hill and put one shaking foot down to rest on the seat for a moment. She pushed back her floppy bush hat—once her father's snap-brimmed bush hat—and let it hang from the string around her throat as she pulled the water bottle from its holder on the bike frame. She only took a few drops, holding them in her mouth to wet the saliva paste that clung to her tongue. She had breathed in enough dust that her mouth tasted like the red clay of the trail. In her younger days, she had taken enough headers to know that taste well, earthy but metallic. It always fought her attempts to rinse it away. She knew now not to even bother. She'd be tasting clay until she was in town. But then she could have a tall glass of darkly sweet jolo. The jolo's effervescence would take the taste of road clay out of her mouth even before the sugar-and-caffeine high started hitting her.

She slipped the bottle back in the holder and re-gripped the handlebars, but paused as the sun behind her finally crested the hill, spilling its golden rays down the far side with its sparse covering of crabgrass, then down to the prairie below. The grain was fully ripe, knocking away its own chaff as the heads atop the stalks rasped together, filling the air with dust that sparkled in the sunlight. The fields themselves looked like they were on fire; the stalks darkened to a dusky red and the heads of grain a brilliant orange. The colors started to mute even as Scout watched, the sun behind her rising ever higher.

For a moment, it was quite beautiful. Breathtaking, even.

But it wouldn't last. Another hour or two and it would be too hot to move out here, the world nothing but a yellow-white glare. Scout wiped her forehead on the dirty sleeve of her faded shirt—also once her father's—then carefully replaced her hat, drawing the string tight under her chin. Then she turned on the bike seat to look back down the way she'd come, whistling low and loud.

Girl appeared first, her oversized paws sounding like a horse galloping on the hard-packed road. Scout had no idea what mix of dogs had made her, but the parts didn't seem to be cohering particularly well, and she suspected her parents had been very differently sized. Girl ran up to Scout and touched her nose to Scout's knee but danced away before Scout could bend over and pet her head, running back the way she'd come and hunkering low on the side of the path. The clod of crabgrass in front of her nose was nowhere near large enough to conceal her, and her glossy black fur stood out starkly against the red of the clay and the grayish green of the sparse plants around her. Girl didn't seem to realize any of this. She radiated confidence in her success at not being seen.

Girl wasn't the brightest of dogs.

At last Shadow appeared, a trim rat terrier with the black spot that covered the top half of his head making him look like he was wearing a bandit mask, albeit a bandit mask that included two cinnamon-colored eyebrows. The white fur on most of his body was untouched by the dust that coated every centimeter of Scout's sweaty body. Scout knew if she slapped Girl's sides that the air would fill with a reddish cloud of clay dust, but not Shadow's. That dog was a master at staying clean.

At least that had been true before Girl had come along.

He knew she was there, his trotting steps slowing as he approached the top of the hill. The path was too narrow to avoid her, and he slowed nearly to a stop, then changed his mind and decided to try for a sprint. Girl hopped out from behind the crabgrass. Shadow twisted to avoid her tackle and continue his trot to Scout's side, but he failed to avoid the black paw that descended onto his back, leaving one large red footprint on his otherwise pristine fur.

"Sorry, buddy," Scout said, brushing him off and unhooking the other bottle from the back of her bike seat, letting him take a few licks from the end before giving Girl a chance. "You guys ready?"

Shadow licked his lips but then froze, ears perked. Scout paused as well, trying to hear what had put Shadow on alert. There was the rustle of the barest of breezes through the crabgrass—or was that a breeze? She listened to the rustle, felt the scarce stirring of air over her hot skin, and wasn't sure they matched.

Slowly she straightened, took the dogs' bottle away, and set a foot on the pedal, ready to send herself down the steep slope but not pushing off just yet. Girl looked at Shadow, who was still on high alert, every muscle in his body flexed tight, his tail quivering. He took a step forward and Girl followed, but then he stopped again and she sat, looking back at Scout for guidance.

Scout gripped the handlebars, but her hurry to get across the prairie before the heat of the day was gone from her mind.

Rebels hid in these hills. She had never seen them, but everyone knew this was where they lurked, waiting for their moment. Scout had been crossing these hills delivering packages and messages for six years now. She knew every slope of these hills, near the path but also further north, where the hills got higher and rockier. There were caves in those taller hills. She had sheltered in them more than once, waiting for killing heat or drenching rain to pass. She had seen signs of other travelers in some, abandoned food packaging, the remains of a fire, once even a perfectly good blanket left behind in a dark corner. She still carried that blanket with her in her saddlebags.

But she had never seen a rebel.

Scout made a slow scan of the world around her, eyes searching every shadow, every suggestion of a hollow in the slope of the hill. There weren't many jobs that took her out this way, and she jumped on everyone she could. The rebels watched these roads; they had seen her dozens of times now. They must have formed some opinion of her, her obvious usefulness as both a messenger that passed unnoticed and an acquirer of hard-to-find things. Was this the day they finally approached her? She was sixteen now. Surely they would approach her soon...

Shadow gave a low growl, so deep in his throat it was a vibration she felt more than heard. He took another cautious step and Scout unsnapped the cargo pocket on her right thigh, eyes still sweeping the desolate world around her as her fingers chose one of the round, perfectly-sized stones. She pulled her slingshot out of its loop at the back of her shorts and set the stone in place, drawing back the band but leaving the weapon only half-raised as Shadow's growl first faded, then resumed with even more intensity.

Girl had lain in the red clay dust to wait for something to happen but she sat up again now, smelling the air in the direction Shadow was slowly stalking towards. Shadow growled again, but Girl drowned him out with a single bark. She was still a puppy, not yet grown into her monstrously huge paws, all awkward gait and floppy ears, but her bark was deep and fierce, as if she were a hound from hell. It made every hair on Scout's body stand on end, and she wasn't even the one being barked at.

"I know someone's there," Scout called, although she wasn't sure of that at all. Sometimes the dogs got all hyped up over nothing. That usually ended in Shadow's repeated barking annoying Girl so much that she wrestled him into silence.

There was no answer and Shadow's growl faded off to nothing, although he was still clenching all of his muscles. Girl flopped back down, watching Shadow closely in case he started barking again and she had to tackle him.

The sun pricked hotly at her shoulders, and Scout put the stone back in her pocket and tucked the slingshot away. She was about to call the dogs' attention back to her when suddenly Shadow was barking like mad, charging forward. There was a runnel, the scar from a past torrent of rain that cut down the hillside, twisting through larger tufts of grass. He raced downhill to the thickest of the tufts and Girl followed, barking her deepest hellhound bark. Scout fumbled for her slingshot, but it was tangled in her shirt and she had to look away from her dogs to free it.

She jerked the slingshot loose from her shirt, got the stone back in the pouch, and raised it to fire all inside of one panicked breath.

The dogs were standing their ground, barking like mad.

The grass shook, and a woman appeared, but not a woman Scout had ever seen before. No, she would've definitely remembered this person. Not because she was taller and broader across the shoulders than most of the men Scout knew. And not because of the braid of copper-colored hair that swung past her hips, a braid thicker than Scout's wrist that lit up in the sun like the grain fields below.

No, it was the clothes. Not even the richest families in the city had such clothes. The sleek shininess of her leather pants showed not a bit of dust clinging to them despite the fact that she had just been crouching in a ditch. The long white shirt that covered her from neck to wrist and down to her knees was equally unsullied, almost too bright to look at in the sunlight. The fabric was opaque enough to keep the sun off, but floated around her in the barely perceptible breeze like she had spun it out of a cloud. She pushed back a wide-brimmed hat, and if she was looking at Scout or the dogs, Scout couldn't tell because she wore two round lenses just large enough to cover her eyes, their surfaces reflective like mirrors. No frames that Scout could see, just lenses right in front of her eyes.

The woman stepped out of the ditch, the shirt billowing behind her but not quite tangling on the brambles that grew on the edge of the ditch. Two belts crisscrossed over her hips, both covered with more gadgets than Scout had ever seen. She couldn't possibly guess at the use of more than a few of them, but they all looked perfectly new, just like the clothes.

No one on the surface had so much tech, so much new of anything. Not even the Space Farers, when they came down to the surface, had such beautiful things. She was like a goddess sprung to life out of the side of the hill.

The woman rested her hands on her hips, near enough to those gadgets but not reaching for anything. Not yet. Scout kept her sling-shot aimed at the woman's throat. The woman raised her hands palms forward but still kept them in easy reach of those belts.

"Well, kid," she said, her voice throaty with a hint of sarcastic humor. "You got me."

2

DESPITE THE HEAT of the sun, the four of them seemed frozen in time. Scout held her slingshot raised high, one foot on the ground and the other still on a pedal, prepared to start rolling down the hill and let inertia take her out into the cover of the prairie grasses. The woman was still half in the tall grasses at the edge of the runnel, long shirt dancing in breezes that Scout didn't feel. Shadow was trembling all over in nervous excitement, sheer joy at finding something to bark at that even Girl had to respect was potentially a legitimate threat. Girl had checked her forward momentum at the sudden appearance of the woman, forelegs braced and back legs nearly sitting in a patch of crabgrass.

Scout tasted the salt of her own sweat running from her forehead to pool at the corner of her mouth. She was going to need another drink soon, a drink and a rest out of the sun's glare. Another drop slipped down, burning at the edge of her eye, but she didn't dare lower the slingshot for even the split second it would take to wipe that sweat away. Her vision blurred, but the woman's lenses flared so brightly she was still confident of her aim.

The first of the daytime insects started its scratchy song and others joined in until a droning chorus built around them, screeching louder and louder before fading back into a silence that was broken by Shadow's resumed barking, yipping over and over as he bounced, crouched, and bounced again.

Scout didn't answer, just kept her slingshot trained on the woman. The woman shrugged and bent forward, hands extended for the dogs to smell. Shadow recoiled, still barking, but Girl found the gesture entirely too frightening and ran back up the hill to cower beside Scout's leg.

Scout cursed under her breath. The hellhound illusion was completely shattered now.

The woman murmured something to Shadow, leaving her hand extended until he finally crept closer and gave her a sniff. Then he sat down and let her pet him.

"Traitor," Scout said. "She didn't even bribe you with food."

"I'm not looking for trouble," the woman said. "I was hoping you'd just pass by and we could both go our separate ways."

"What are you doing out here?" Scout asked, still not lowering her weapon.

"None of your business," the woman said amiably. "And you?"

"The same," Scout shot back.

"No reason we can't both get back to it, then," the woman said. Shadow was jumping to get her attention, higher and higher in those rat-terrier bounds he had. She laughed and caught him in both hands at the apex of yet another leap, keeping him still as she scratched his ears.

Scout pulled the stone back further in the slingshot as she whistled a high, brief note. Shadow pulled away from the woman's grasp and ran to Scout's side to sit at rigid attention, not even breaking when Girl swiped at him with one clumsy paw. He had lapsed badly, but he remembered his training now.

"I'm not looking to hurt you," the woman said, less amiable now. "You can put your weapon away."

"I don't think so," Scout said, keeping careful aim. Her forearm was beginning to ache but not yet tremble.

The woman sighed and reached behind her own back. She brought out a laser pistol but let it dangle from one fingertip, just showing it to her, not threatening her with it.

"You might as well, kid," the woman said, spinning the pistol around her finger, catching it, spinning it the other way. Scout kept the stone pulled back. The woman spun the pistol up in the air, caught it, then slipped it back out of sight behind her back and raised both of her palms to Scout. "Come on, be reasonable."

Scout fought back a slight trembling of her arm. She couldn't tell, not being able to see the woman's eyes, but she was sure the woman had seen. The corner of her mouth was pulling up ever so slightly. Scout released her held breath with a whoosh and lowered the sling-shot. But she kept it in one hand, the stone in the other.

She wasn't going to be as fast as that woman with her pistol, even with everything ready in her hands. Having watched that woman spinning a pistol around, she almost doubted she could release the stone from the firing position faster than the stranger could draw and shoot. Even if she got a shot off, the woman would just dodge out of the stone's path.

The woman stepped closer and something in the way she moved said she was even more ready for sudden action than Shadow was in his full muscle-clenching alert mode. She looked like something more than human, or other than, and Scout didn't think it would be possible to overestimate what she could do.

Scout fetched her bottle and sucked another few drops into her mouth. She probably should just collect her dogs and go, but leaving without knowing what this woman was up to would drive her mad. No one came to these hills except her and the rebels. Everyone else traveling between the two cities took the ferry around the point. Scout made a nice enough living moving things over land that people wanted delivered without questions from officials or intrusive inspections. She knew what she did was not technically legal, although she was very good at playing dumb when caught. And it'd been years since she'd been caught.

This woman had nothing sizable on her. She could be delivering a message, as Scout sometimes did, but she doubted that was what she was doing. No one dressed so finely delivered messages.

"Are you looking for the rebels?" Scout asked.

"Why, do you know where they are?" the woman asked, that slight quirk back to the corner of her mouth.

"No, no more than anyone else knows," Scout said. "Everyone knows they're in the hills."

"Indeed, I had heard that," the woman said. "But your local politics aren't really my concern."

"Local?" Scout repeated. "They are organizing to destroy the Space Farers. That's global politics."

"To be sure," the woman said. "Local to this globe."

Scout's mind boggled. Where was this woman from?

"I can help you find the rebels," Scout offered. There couldn't be another reason for a stranger to be out this far from the cities. And she was so out of the ordinary, surely someone would come out of hiding to confront them.

"You said you don't know where they are," the woman said.

"No, but I know where they're not. That can shorten your search."

"It's kind of you to offer, but I've got this," the woman said. "And again, not here for your little rebellion."

"But you're a Space Farer, aren't you?" Scout's eyes swept over the woman's outfit another time. "You must be."

"Everyone who isn't a Planet Dweller is a Space Farer," the woman said, not a question. Scout nodded but stopped as the woman shook her head with a sad smile. "No, there are many, many more people in the universe than fit in your two little groups."

"But if you're not from here, why are you here now?"

"I'm not the only one here not from here," the woman said.

Scout frowned. Was she talking about Scout? Well, she wasn't from the prairie, but the city she was from no longer existed, so it wasn't so odd to find her where she wasn't from, was it?

Or was she talking about someone else? Scout opened her mouth to speak when something on one of the woman's belts beeped and she glanced down at it. She frowned and tapped it to make it stop beeping, then stepped up to the top of the ridge next to Scout on her bike. She changed the angle of her hat to block out the midmorning sun and looked down the path that wound through a steep channel snaking back and forth on the far side of the hill. Girl looked up at her, her tail thumping loudly in the dust.

"I need to get going, kid," the woman said. "You're heading back to the capital?"

"Maybe," Scout said.

"Perhaps I'll see you again before I head out, then. I'll probably have some time to kill waiting for my ride to come pick me up. What's your name?"

"Scout."

"You messing with me, kid? That's not a name, it's an occupation," the woman said, mouth quirking again.

"I don't scout, I deliver. And Scout is my name."

"Suit yourself, Scout."

"And you?"

"You can call me Warrior," the woman said, and Scout had no doubt that wasn't remotely close to her real name. The woman turned the full glare of those mirrored lenses on Scout, but Scout refused to play along.

"Warrior," she repeated, as if it were the most normal name in the world. "Pleased to meet you."

"And your dogs?"

"That's Shadow," Scout said, still annoyed at Shadow's betrayal.

"And this one?"

"Girl," Scout admitted. "She's not really mine."

"She seems like yours," Warrior said.

"Shadow is my dog. I trained him from a pup. My father helped before he... well. Shadow has been with me for six years now. Girl, she just turned up one day a month or so ago. Shadow and I were camping near a mining town and when we woke up, she was just there, curled up with us like she was part of our family. Haven't been able to get rid of her since, she just follows us everywhere. She's not that bright, barely trainable. Not much point giving her a name. I'm sure she's just going to wander off again at some point."

"I see," Warrior said. There was an undertone to her voice, like what she was agreeing to was not quite what Scout had said. Scout was about to call her out for being condescending when another one of

Warrior's belt gadgets started beeping urgently. Warrior pulled it off the belt and silenced it, frowning at the screen on the device.

Something else was beeping too, something in Scout's saddlebags. She twisted on the bike seat to reach behind her. She only had one electronic device, one thing that would beep, and she always kept it in easy reach in a separate pouch sewn in the top band between the two bags.

Sometimes it went off for no reason, cheap piece of crap that it was, but Scout was certain this wasn't one of those times. Not if Warrior's had gone off too. Still, she forced herself to swallow back the rising panic and look at the dial.

The needle was buried beyond the red zone. She had seen it flirt with the darker edge of the orange zone, but it never moved so far as to touch the red zone. Certainly never passed into it.

"Solar flare," she said, her voice a dry croak.

"Coronal mass ejection. Or, as you say, solar flare," Warrior agreed, putting the device back on her belt. "Well, kid—or, rather, Scout—time to run for our lives, yeah?"

3

SCOUT LOOKED TO THE HILLS. There were caves they could shelter in, but would they be deep enough for a flare of this magnitude?

She looked out over the prairie. The dome of the capital city was easy to spot, the midmorning sun reflecting back like a second, setting sun. But the brightness was deceptive; it was much farther away than it looked. They could never get to it in time.

In between where she was perched on her bike on the hilltop and the nearest city gate was nothing but grain, kilometer after kilometer of nodding grasses that might keep the sun off for the hottest hours of the day but would do nothing against a rain of charged particles punching through the magnetic shielding the original colonists had installed in space before making planetfall. The sun these days was throwing off ever-larger ejections, these shield-overwhelming proton storms becoming more and more frequent.

But never anything close to this.

"We have to get to shelter," Warrior said, clipping her gadget back on her belt and regarding Scout's bike. It wasn't the bike her father had given her oh so many years ago. That bike had been partly motorized, with wide tires capable of carrying heavier loads. But two years ago, she'd hit a growth spurt that made pedaling that thing awkward as hell. She had traded for a larger but less tricked-out bike: no motor, tires adequate for the hilly terrain she biked over, but not meant for heavy loads.

Warrior threw a leg over the rack that supported the saddlebags and the back tire nearly flattened beneath her weight.

"What are you made of, iron?" Scout asked.

"Never mind, let's get going," Warrior said. "Lean over the handlebars and I'll lean over you, distribute the weight better."

"Sure," Scout said. The vision of the two of them screaming across the prairie with the cannonball speed their combined weight was going to generate gripped her mind, but she ignored it, leaning over the handlebars and pushing off.

Warrior's long legs kept them from tipping over, her toes brushing over the ground as Scout worked the pedals. Then, all too quickly, momentum took them and they were rolling, bouncing over the uneven ground, flying into the air when they launched off a rock and landing hard but not slowing. For the first third of the slope, the dogs kept up with them, running with tongues lolling and then with mouths closed as they focused on their sprinting. Then it was only Shadow who kept up, his lithe form working with total efficiency. But at last even he fell behind, out of Scout's view.

The bike raced along the narrow track between two endless fields of grain. Scout had taken her feet off the pedals during the descent but she put them back now, first matching the pace their momentum had set and then adding muscle on the downstrokes to keep them moving.

But soon the momentum was gone, and she was just pedaling hard. She kept it up as long as she could, but Warrior was extraordinarily heavy and Scout, who always carefully matched her efforts to the amount of water she'd be able to hydrate with, started to feel lightheaded and regretted every drop of moisture she was losing in sweat.

"Stop," Warrior said close to her ear, and Scout readily complied, all but flopping over her handlebars. Warrior swung off the back of the bike, another device in her hand. She kept her eyes glued on the tiny screen of the device as she made a slow 360. Scout fought to get her breath under control and tipped her head to look back behind her, anxious for a glimpse of her dogs. Shadow knew the road well and

Girl would stay with him. They would catch up, but she didn't like not having them in her sights.

The sky brightened, the prairie building up toward the white-hot intensity it would reach at midday, but this was more than that. Scout held the brim of her hat to block the light of the sun and gazed up at the rest of the sky. Yes, she could see them now, the occasional streaks of white light arcing across the sky, but more now than she'd ever seen before. The shield was still working, protecting the planet below from the worst of the flare, but not all of it.

"We're not going to make it," Scout said. "I can't pedal us both back to the capital in time."

"We don't need to get to the capital," Warrior said, eyes still on her gadget.

"I hate to break it to you, but there's nothing else out here. Nothing but grass. Maybe we should've tried for a cave," she said miserably. No way was she pedaling back up that hill now.

"You know those all would've been too small," Warrior said. Scout felt a sudden chill. Had the strange woman been reading her mind? She wasn't looking at her now, although even if she were, Scout would get no read on her, not with those lenses over her eyes.

"So what, then?" Scout asked. She looked back again and her heart did a happy leap as Shadow came into view, too tired to sprint but still managing a brisk trot. She looked at her own solar flare warning device, cheap as it was. "We usually get more warning than this. Why would that change? It's not like the sun got any closer."

"Good question for a later time," Warrior said. "This way."

"What way?" Scout asked, but when Warrior plunged into the field south of them, Scout followed, leaning back as she slowly pedaled. Shadow had seen where she was going, and Scout was certain the dark smudge at the edge of her vision back up the trail was Girl, plodding along after him.

Warrior kept marching forward, gadget in her hand held high. The sky over them was filling with more and more streaks, and Scout tipped her head so that the brim of her hat blocked all that from view. Those were the particles the shield was actually catching. The ones getting through, those were silent and invisible. They could be bombarding her body right now and she wouldn't know. Penetrating her bones, making subtle changes in her marrow that would mean cancer years from now.

And that was just the slow death she could look forward to if she got out of the storm now.

"Where are we going?" Scout asked, looking back at the wake her bike was leaving behind, grass bent by the passage of her handlebars, broken stalks trampled under Warrior's feet and her tires. The dogs were in the grass too now; Shadow apparently had waited at the edge for Girl to catch up and the two were walking shoulder to shoulder, noses close to the ground as if they needed the scent trail to find her.

"Catching a ride," Warrior said, pushing through the last row of grain and emerging into a clearing in the center of the field. The grass had been smoothed down in a large circle.

"Is this where you landed?" Scout asked, looking around the perimeter of the circle. Nothing but grass all around them, but here it had been almost gently flattened over, the grass still growing, the stalks bent but not broken.

"Are you kidding? Do you see scorch marks?"

"Then what is this place?" Scout asked.

"Hell if I know," Warrior said.

"Then why—"

Warrior raised a finger, needlessly as Scout had already fallen silent, head tipped as she listened to a distant rumble. Farm equipment? She hoped there would be room enough for both of them and the dogs along with the farmer. Only what farmer would still be out in an active solar flare?

"There," Warrior said, raising her gadget high once more as the rumble drew closer.

"What is that thing?" Scout asked, pointing her chin at the gadget. Warrior grinned, one side of her mouth quirking up more than the other.

"I use it to catch rides," she said.

"Like hitchhiking?"

"More like commandeering," Warrior said, lowering the gadget as the rumble grew louder still, sounding for a brief moment like it was coming from all around them. Then the top of a rover came into view from the depths of the fields to the south of them, rolling into the clearing and coming to a halt in front of Warrior. Warrior reached out, patted the nose of the vehicle, and put the gadget back in its place on her belt.

"Neat trick," Scout said, leaning back on her bicycle seat to take in the sight of the rover from nose to stern. She'd seen something similar back in her school days in a sim, but never in real life. The original colonizers had used rovers like this for long-range scouting missions. A half-dozen colonists could fit inside with supplies enough to last them for months without having to go outside. "Nice choice."

"Luck," Warrior said, walking around the side of the rover to the door on its side. "I just summoned the nearest thing that was moving."

"Do we knock?"

"You'd think that would be redundant, given how I brought them here," Warrior said, but she pushed back her hat to look up the length of the door before rapping her knuckles on the metal. The rover was like a shuttle on wheels, larger and thicker hulled than the vehicles in routine use on the planet these days. Aside from the trains and ferries that ran from city to city, transportation planetside was bicycle, auto-rickshaw, or your own two feet.

"Your gun won't penetrate that," Scout said after what was more than a reasonable wait for a response from within.

"Don't need a gun," Warrior said, grabbing something else from her belt. She set it under the door panel and it pulled itself the last bit of the way to the metal hull to land with a metallic clang. Something magnetic, Scout guessed. Warrior touched a fingertip to it like she was trying to encourage a small animal to do something in exchange for a bit of food. There was a soft whir and then a louder clang as the door unsealed, moving several centimeters forward, hinges and all, and then stopping.

"Let's get inside," Warrior said, retrieving her device from under the door panel. "Sling your bike into the cargo hatch there between the treads in back. Come, dogs!"

The dogs looked up at her but didn't follow, preferring to stay close to Scout as she dismounted her bike and shoved it inside the narrow space in the back between the wide treads and under the rover floor. If there was anything else inside, she saw no sign of it. She shut the door with a little click, then ran around the side to the door Warrior had left hanging wide open. The dogs followed close at her heels but hesitated at the sharp step up to get inside.

"Hurry it," Warrior said, close at hand but quite out of sight in the shadowy darkness of the rover's interior, especially to Scout's sun-dazzled eyes. Scout bent and scooped Girl up into her arms, hoisting her up to the doorway. Shadow was half Girl's weight but needed not a bit of help. Once he understood what Scout wanted, he leapt neatly inside, nails scrabbling on the metal floor as he disappeared further inside. Scout gripped the handhold in the doorway and pulled herself up after them. She felt Warrior reach past her to pull the door shut. Then the door on its own rolled into Scout's backside as it resealed itself, hinges once more tucked away as the edge of the door over-lapped the doorway and all four sides.

Scout pressed her hands back against the door, sensing the presence of others in the rover but forced to wait for her eyes to adjust. Warrior with her neat little reflective lenses could probably see as clearly as ever, but for the moment Scout was quite blind. Blind among strangers.

And at least one of them was someone Shadow didn't like.

4

WHEN SCOUT'S eyes started to adjust, she could make out Shadow's form first. His name had always been a misnomer; with that brightly white fur, he glowed in dark places like a ghost. Or at least like a ghost with a few dark patches, wearing a bandit mask to obscure its eyes. He was standing, muscles rigid, the hair over his spine standing on end like a dinosaur's bony ridge.

Scout realized she was still standing in a doorway that created a niche off the main body of the rover's interior, the one open spot along the windowless walls, and stepped out from between the two cabinets that bracketed the space. Warrior had moved all the way inside and was leaning one hip against a counter that was part of a kitchenette with a microwave over a tiny sink and a little bit of countertop over the mini-fridge. Behind her, against the back wall of the rover, was a stack of bunk beds, each large enough to hold two people if they were a bit friendly.

Warrior's mood was still undetectable, her eyes hidden by the reflective lenses, but Scout could see she was staring down someone in the front of the rover and followed her gaze past a cluttered table—even the built-in benches were covered in an array of tablets, half-disassembled appliances, and machine components—to a woman holding an electric prod, the kind used to get livestock to move along. She was alternating aiming it at Warrior and at the still-growling Shadow. Behind her was another woman, further in the front of the cabin of the rover and a few steps up. Her hands were on the cattle prod woman's shoulders, but whether to restrain her or to encourage her, Scout couldn't guess.

The woman in front looked decades older than Warrior, with silver hair cut short and bristling up off her scalp. Her deeply sun-damaged skin together with the prod in her hand suggested a life out on the ranches far to the south—farther than Scout had ever gone on her bike, although she would encounter the drovers in town from time to time and knew the look.

The woman behind her was also advanced in years, but with paler skin and salt-and-pepper streaks in the hair she wore tied in a tail at the nape of her neck that ended in a blunt edge just below her shoulder blades. Her hands squeezed the other woman's shoulders and the other woman moved the end of the prod, aiming it down at the still-growling Shadow, then back up to Warrior again. Warrior's arms were crossed loosely, the picture of unconcern.

The air inside the rover was much cooler and Scout pushed the hat back off her head, letting it dangle from the string tied under her chin as she ran her hands through her sweat-drenched curls. The cold air felt so good on her scalp.

Now she just needed a drink. Jolo would be divine, but water would do. She eyed the mini-fridge Warrior was leaning against and wondered what was inside.

"Shut up that dog," the woman with the prod said. Warrior gave Scout a nod.

"Hush, Shadow," Scout said, catching the dog's collar and running a hand over his head. Shadow gave another growl, this one with more of a questioning tone, then looked up at Scout. Scout petted him again and the hairs on his back lay down.

"We're not looking for trouble," Warrior said. "Just needed a lift."

"You just hijacked our rover," the woman said, eyes narrowing.

"Yes, I did," Warrior said without apology. "But it's not going to be enough, is it?"

Scout felt a chill run up her spine that had nothing to do with the coolness of the air. What did she mean, not enough?

"No, it isn't," the woman without the prod said. "Not this time."

"What are we talking about?" the woman with the prod asked before Scout could.

"Your hull," Warrior said. "It's not enough." She uncrossed her arms, retrieved her alert device, and showed the screen to the two women. Scout leaned in to take a look at it. The screen rotated through a series of images, measuring current intensity, then a future forecast of intensity reaching a number Scout's cheaper device didn't even have on its dial.

Then a duration prediction.

"Four days?" the woman said, lowering the prod as she leaned closer to the little screen. "Four days, at that level?"

"Best estimate," Warrior said as she put the device back on her belt. "We need to get under a dome."

"Too far," the woman at the top of the stairs said, turning to disappear inside what Scout guessed was the cockpit.

"Underground then," Warrior said, more loudly so her voice could carry up the stairs. She gave the woman with the prod a pointed look. The woman raised the prod again, fingers gripping tightly enough to turn her knuckles white, but then changed her mind and shoved the prod aside, tossing it onto the tabletop and sending bits of equipment raining down over the benches to the floor. She spun and pulled herself up into the cockpit, sliding into the seat opposite the one her companion was already in. Warrior climbed up after, putting a hand on the back of each seat to lean in and watch what the women were doing on the panels.

Scout crept closer but couldn't see the displays, only the reactions on the women's faces. There was more light here, a watery sort of sunlight penetrating through thick panes of scratched glass set in a narrow band around the top of the cockpit. A person standing between the seats could see in all directions from there, if just along the horizon.

"We'll never make it to any of the cities before that intensity spike," the woman in the driver's seat said. "This buggy wasn't exactly built for speed. The hull might be able to handle the worst of it—"

"No, not remotely," Warrior said.

The woman looked back at her. "You're not from here," she said.

"Obviously. But I'm not unfamiliar with coronal mass ejections."

"Can you get this rover up in the mountains?" Scout asked. "I know some caves."

"Big enough to fit this beast inside?" the woman who had held the prod asked.

"Maybe—"

"No good," Warrior said. "Anything with an opening we could drive through would be too open."

"But you said underground," Scout said. "There isn't anything else out here."

"Isn't there?" Warrior asked the two women. They looked over all their panels and shrugged.

"We're a bit outside of our usual stomping grounds, but nothing is on any of the registered maps, and nothing is pinging on any of the comm channels."

"Let me," Warrior said, moving to put a knee down between the two seats. She took something off her belt and plugged it into a jack.

"That's what I meant," the woman in the driver's seat said. "Your tech. You're not from here."

"Yeah, how did you hijack our rover?"

"I have access to certain overrides," Warrior said. Scout could see maps from the screen on the panel reflecting off her lenses, zooming in and spinning and zooming out again.

"How? We've owned this rover for decades now. It hasn't been serviced in years. When did you install an exploit? How?" The prod woman looked at her wit's end, raking hands over her close-cropped hair. "Blazing stars, *why* would you?"

"It's not you," Warrior said, still focused on the maps. "The exploit exists in all vehicles of all types and I have access to it."

"Who are you?" the woman demanded.

"Leave it be, Ottilie," the woman in the driver's seat said calmly.

"But—"

"Just leave it for later," she said again.

Ottilie slumped back in her seat, still fuming but now silent.

"There," Warrior said, pointing at something on the panel.

"What is it?" the older woman asked, leaning closer.

"A landing beacon. Very old-school, probably been there for decades, pinging away."

"What good does that do us?" Ottilie asked. Scout could tell by the tight grip of her hands on the armrests how hard she was fighting to keep the abrasiveness out of her tone. "A landing field?"

"No, look," the other woman said. "The signal is coming from underground. At least a dozen meters underground. That will be good. That will be enough."

"What if we can't get down there?" Ottilie asked.

"You know this place?" the woman asked.

Ottilie leaned in to look closer at the map, but shook her head. "No. This isn't my neighborhood."

"What about you, Scout?" Warrior asked, turning her body sideways so Scout could lean past her. She looked at the flashing light in the center of the map, then found a few other landmarks to orient herself.

"I've been near there," she said. "Never seen anything but grainfields."

"It's our best bet," Warrior said. "Set the course."

The driver nodded and started pressing buttons. Ottilie's eyes opened wide, but she said nothing. The rover beneath them lurched back to life, turning around three quarters of a circle before straightening out and lumbering ahead at a somewhat faster speed.

"Set the auto," Warrior said. "We should ride this out in the back. More shielding."

"Yes," the woman agreed, pushing more buttons. Warrior tapped Scout's shoulder and Scout crawled backwards, back down to where the dogs waited. Girl had flopped down in the door niche, fast asleep, but Shadow was still standing, looking around with little jerks of his head from object of interest to object of interest.

"What do you think it is?" Scout asked as Warrior gathered up the junk on one of the benches and set it on the counter in the kitchenette so she could sit at the cluttered table and consult one of her gadgets.

"I already said, landing beacon. Old model, probably like this rover from the first wave of planetfall before the colonization got underway."

"Is that a coincidence?" Scout asked.

"Well, yeah," Warrior said, directing those blank lenses Scout's way briefly before looking back down at the device in her hands. "Solar flares and killer heat aside, your planet is quite tech friendly. Calm weather, nothing particularly corrosive in the atmosphere. No reason for things to fail."

Scout gathered up an array of plugs, piling them back in a plastic crate and setting it on the floor so she could sit across from Warrior. She cast a glance at the mini-fridge. "Any jolo in there?"

"Jolo? Haven't had that in years," Ottilie said. She had come to the bottom of the stairs but was leaning against the doorframe, arms crossed as she glowered at the intruders at her table.

"Water then?" Scout asked.

"We have water," the driver said, brushing past Ottilie to head to the kitchenette. Ottilie scowled but turned to pull the hatch shut, blocking out what little light came through the band of windows. She spun the lock until it engaged with a grinding clang.

"Here," the driver said, giving a little smile as she set a glass of cool, clear water in front of Scout. "I'll get a bowl for your dogs."

"Thanks," Scout said, taking a cautious sip. She'd expected the faintly metallic taste of water from a recycler, but was surprised by the crisp, clean taste of it. "Fresh?"

"Bottled from the glaciers at the pole," she said. "I like to splurge on the little luxuries."

Scout took another sip. It didn't have the caffeine/sugar double whammy of jolo, but it did get the clay taste out of her mouth.

"How long?" Warrior asked, not looking up from her gadget.

"An hour," the driver said. "Assuming no obstacles."

"I think it's time you told us who you are," Ottilie said.

"Just a stranger caught out in the storm," Warrior said. "The kid and I needed a ride to safety, and you were all that was in range. I'd apologize for the inconvenience, but clearly without me here to locate that beacon for you, you'd have been trapped out in it as well. You would've lasted a day or two longer, but not through the whole storm."

"That still might happen," Ottilie said. "What if we get to this beacon hidden underground and can't get down to it? What are we going to do, dig?"

"One thing at a time," Warrior said. "Do you have shielding suits?"

"Two," the driver said. "They're old."

"Can I see them?"

The driver turned to head to the back but Ottilie caught her arm, holding her still while she stared Warrior down. "Still didn't catch your name."

Warrior didn't look up.

"I'm Scout," Scout said to break the silence. "The rat terrier is Shadow. The other one is Girl."

"Ebba," the driver said, putting out a hand for Scout to shake. "And this is Ottilie."

"She's Warrior," Scout said, indicating the woman across the table from her with the tip of her head. "Pretty sure that's a fake name, but mine is real."

"So are ours," Ottilie said, narrowing suspicious eyes at the oblivious Warrior. Ebba murmured something, brushing Ottilie's hand off her arm. This time, she let her go.

"Where does one get a device like that to summon rovers to rescue you, whether their drivers are so inclined or not?"

"This doesn't do that," Warrior said, thumbs running over buttons on the front of her device. "If you're interested in such an item, getting closer to the galactic center would be a good start."

Ottilie snorted, crossing her arms and slouching back against the closed cockpit door. "You're from outside the system? No way. The Space Farers would never let you down here without an escort. And once you got here, you'd get another escort of uppity-ups from the governor's people."

"Yes, I'm sure that's true," Warrior said, at last putting the device away.

Ebba draped two shiny suits across the tabletop. Scout could see circuitry lining the interior. She'd never seen one before, not close enough to touch it, but she knew what it was. The first expedition to scout the planet's surface had worn suits like this in the archival videos in her history program. The surface hadn't really been safe until the shield created by the network of satellites up in orbit had been finished, but the first colonizers hadn't wanted to wait for that to be built before starting work on the surface. The suits had been designed to generate their own magnetic shielding to protect against solar particles.

They had only been marginally effective. The scouts had survived their missions, but every one of them had gotten a bunch of funky new cancers for their trouble.

Warrior ran her hands over the suits, looking for imperfections. Her reflective lenses shone up at Scout briefly.

"Don't worry, kid. Two will be enough. We'll just have to take it in shifts."

Scout nodded mutely, then took another long drink of water.

She had no way of knowing, sealed inside the windowless cabin of the rover as she was, but somehow she could just feel it, the sky full of streaks, long trails of solar particles pummeling against the magnetic shield, desperate to get through and rain down on the surface below. Some things there was just no hiding from.

5

THE ROVER ROCKED GENTLY as the auto driver maneuvered over the prairie, wheels dipping in and out of ruts and over exposed stones. Scout let her body fall into a rhythm, rolling with the hypnotic motion. Ebba tidied up the table and benches, gathering all the bits of machinery and tools into totes and stacking them in the back of the rover in the bottom of the two bunks. Scout's brain sleepily observed that this bottom bunk was just a bare mattress. Her eyes traveled up to the top bunk, neatly made up with a faded patchwork quilt spread over it, two pillows under matching quilted covers across the head of the bed.

She looked at Ebba, settling the last of the totes in the bottom bunk. She and Ottilie were both wearing nondescript jumpsuits of faded gray. They probably dated as far back as the rover and the shielded suits, back to the first colonization. The original colonists had come with a large supply of the garments, and given that the fabric was so resistant to damage and even staining, most of them were still in use among Planet Dwellers and Space Farers both. Scout didn't have one, but both of her parents had worn them nearly every day.

Ebba wore hers fastened up to her throat and down to her wrists but had added a shimmering scarf draped loosely around her shoulders, and Scout guessed by the paleness of her skin that she wore it to cover her head and face before going out into the sun. She'd seen other pale people with similar garments and knew the fabric had UV protective properties.

But everyone she'd ever seen with one had been a Space Farer. Everyone she'd ever seen with skin so milky pale had been a Space Farer.

Scout looked over at Ottilie. Her skin was as dark as burnt bread, creased and leathery and flecked all over with darker freckles and moles. She was definitely not a Space Farer. The sleeves of her jumpsuit were cut off at the shoulder, leaving her lean arms bare. There was a military insignia tattooed on her left biceps—not one Scout had ever seen before, but given that the design centered around a big gun, she guessed Ottilie had served on the crew of one of the massive guns that had fired on the Space Farer satellites and stations during the war.

Scout roused out of her half doze when a dog's nails raked over her thigh. She bent down and scooped up Shadow, settling him on her lap. He was just a little too big to cuddle easily anymore, but he had not left the need behind when he ceased being a puppy. She got him situated how he was most comfortable: nose buried in her right armpit, her left arm under his back end to keep him from spilling off her lap. He snuffed out a breath and closed his eyes.

Girl was still flopped on the floor in front of the doorway, four paws all tucked and tangled together. Such huge paws; how could she ever grow into them?

"Slide over," Ottilie said to Scout.

Shadow protested as she moved down the bench, following the right angle to sit with her back against the outer wall of the rover. The plastic under her thighs was cold. Ottilie slid to sit across from Warrior in the spot Scout had just warmed. She folded her hands together and watched Warrior. Warrior had a device shaped like a tablet in her hands, tapping away with her thumbs as if writing a message, but there was no screen of text, no buttons under her thumbs that she could see. But perhaps Warrior could, projected on the inside of those lenses?

Ottilie leaned forward to look at the object in Warrior's hands, the flat featurelessness of it, as if she were holding a thin slab of stone. Ottilie glanced over at Scout and Scout lifted her dog-free shoulder in a shrug.

"Here," Ebba said, setting a basket of hardtack biscuits on the table. "It's not much for flavor, but it will fill your belly, and we have plenty of it."

She reached farther across the table to set a cloth napkin in front of Scout, the cuff of her gray jumpsuit pulling back from her wrist as she stretched. She had a tiny tattoo on her wrist just at the base of her thumb, a simple insignia Scout knew well. The Space Farer military had no separate units or quads or corps with their own branding, just one stylized upside-down V shape meant to suggest the head of a rocket.

"You were both in the military," Scout said.

Ebba turned her hand over, saw her exposed tattoo, and stood back up, smoothing the cuff down over it. "Yes," she said. "A long time ago."

"On different sides," Scout added.

"Like she said, it was a long time ago," Ottilie said.

"What are the two of you doing out here, roaming around together in a rover?" Scout asked.

"Living," Ottilie said as if that one word ended the conversation.

Warrior paused in her typing—perhaps looking up at Ottilie, Scout couldn't tell—then resumed typing without saying a word.

"Together?" Scout persisted.

Ottilie leaned toward Scout, eyes blazing as she started to open her mouth, but shut it again and sat back at the touch of Ebba's hand on her shoulder.

"The war has been over for years now," Ebba said to Scout. "We've earned this peace, and if we choose to enjoy it together, well, we've earned that too."

"But why out here?" Scout asked. "Are you looking for something?"

"Quite the opposite," Ebba said with a soft smile. "We like the solitude."

Scout frowned and reached for a biscuit, setting it on the napkin before crumbling off a bite-sized piece to sneak into her mouth without the napping dog in her lap noticing.

An ancient rover taking them to an equally ancient beacon. Enemies of a decades-long conflict roaming together through the wilds that were Scout's personal domain. It seemed like a lot of coincidences to Scout, and extremely unlikely ones at that.

She had been waiting for the rebels to come for her for years now, but perhaps she had been waiting for the wrong signs. If only her father had told her what to look for when he had sent her away.

She put another bit of biscuit in her mouth, letting it soften on her tongue despite the growling of her awakened stomach.

She closed her eyes and brought that day back to mind, as she often did. If the memory were an object, it would be worn and faded from so much handling. She remembered the sky, the usual washed-out bluish white a deep indigo even seen through the shimmering dome. When her father had stepped out into the courtyard to bring her the lunch her mother had packed for her, he had hesitated in the doorway, eyes up on that sky. What had been that look on his face? Had he been caught in a momentary sense of wonderment, at the rare beauty their home planet's atmosphere so rarely provided for them? Or had he sensed something sinister in it? A warning?

Scout hadn't really noticed any of it at the time, and he had really only paused for the briefest of moments. But every time she returned to the memory, she was more and more sure. He had hesitated, had seen the dark blue of the sky and known it meant something, but he had carefully schooled his features, putting the smile back on his face before handing the still-warm bundle of food to his oldest child.

She didn't know how impending doom could change the color of the sky, but her father must've known something. There must've been a reason he had sent her away, just her and Shadow on her bike with the package for one of her mother's friends in the next city tied neatly to the rack over the back wheel of the bike, the lunch in the basket hanging from the handlebars for when she got halfway across the prairie. It would be nightfall before she reached the city, but her mother's friends would have dinner waiting for her, and a bed for the night, and another lunch for the trip back the next day. She had her father's favorite hat and one of his shirts to protect her from the bright sunlight and she wore them like a young warrior in a fairy tale wore their father's armor on their first quest.

But at midmorning, the sky still that impossible blue, Scout had been blown from her bike by the blast of dirt and debris, Shadow tumbling after her. They had been cut all over, shallow wounds, as it turned out, but the memory of seeing herself bleeding all over, Shadow's white fur streaked with blood as well... that image still was enough to make her breath catch and her eyes wince.

It was only when the dust had settled that she realized what had cut them: the shattered remains of the dome that protected her home city. The dome was gone from the horizon, the buildings too.

Scout had found her bike and put the shivering Shadow into the basket that no longer held her mother's fresh-baked bread, cold meatloaf from the night before, an apple from the tree in the courtyard. All that was gone, lost in the shock wave.

And all that remained of her city was a crater. Her father, her mother, and her little brother had all disappeared.

She had never seen the rock that fell from the sky that day. The asteroid the Space Farers had snagged and hurled down to the surface. The debris-turned-weapon that had changed her life forever.

Her father, he had known. Somehow, he had known and had sent her away.

But why? What was she supposed to be doing? Joining the rebellion, she had always thought, and she had waited years for that to happen.

Scout opened her eyes and reached for another piece of biscuit. Shadow grunted at the movement, but Scout ran a hand down his back and he settled back into his nap.

Warrior was still tapping on the blank tablet, Ottilie still watching her closely. Scout could see her eyes darting back and forth as Warrior's thumbs moved, as if trying to mentally construct a keyboard and read the letters being touched despite them being both upside down and invisible. Judging by the scowl lines around her eyebrows, she wasn't having any luck.

Ebba set a full glass of water in front of Scout and gave her another smile. She seemed very friendly. And Scout couldn't shake the feeling that meeting her now wasn't just a coincidence.

"Did you know my parents?" Scout asked.

"Your parents?" Ebba repeated, her smile twisting into a look of confusion.

The panel on the wall next to the door to the cockpit began to flash and beep softly. Warrior's thumbs finally stilled as they all looked at the flashing light.

"What is it?" Ottilie asked, turning to look back over her shoulder.

"I'll see," Ebba said. "Stay here." She spun the wheel in the hatch and swung the door open, scrambling up the stairs to the cockpit.

Despite her words, both Ottilie and Warrior followed her, leaving Scout once more to linger at the bottom of the steps, unable to get closer to see what was going on, having to try to interpret everything by the way the three of them reacted.

Two of them, actually. Warrior's face never revealed a thing beyond that little quirk of the corner of her mouth when she was amused. And whatever was going on now, it wasn't amusing.

Shadow squirmed, and Scout set him on the floor. Girl lifted her head to look at both of them, then flopped back down to continue her nap.

"Do you see it?" Ebba asked.

"See what?" Scout asked. Ottilie was in the other seat now, looking over the panels on her side of the cockpit. Warrior was on the top step, raising herself up on tiptoes to look through the narrow band of windows.

"There," she said, pointing. Ebba and Ottilie both stood to peer out the window in the direction Warrior was indicating.

"What is it?" Scout asked with rising impatience.

"Wow," Ottilie said. "That's new. Quite flash."

"Is it?" Warrior asked, sounding less impressed.

Scout was going to go mad.

"It looks like they jumped that rock there," Ebba said, pointing. "See the gouges on the surface? They must've damaged their vehicle. That's why it's parked here."

"There's someone inside," Warrior said.

"I don't see—" Ottilie began, squinting.

"Two someones. A woman and a child," Warrior said.

"I see them now," Ebba said. "The woman is waving at us."

"You must be right, they broke down here," Ottilie said.

"We have room enough for two more. We should stop," Warrior said.

"And open the door again?" Ottilie demanded.

"Briefly," Warrior said.

"We have the suits," Scout said.

"Not necessary. Ebba, pull up right next to them. They can jump from their town car to the rover; it will only take a second."

Scout took hold of the hem of Warrior's shirt. It felt just as filmy soft as it looked, sliding through her fingers like a dream. She pulled it to one side to get a look at the one gadget on Warrior's belt she knew the purpose of: the solar flare detector.

They were well within the red zone.

Warrior felt Scout's hand on her shirt and turned to fix those reflective lenses on her. "Only a second. It will be all right."

"It's weird. Two more people out here in the middle of nowhere."

"It's just a coincidence, kid," Warrior said.

Ebba disabled the auto driver and took over the controls, hands on the steering yoke and feet working over pedals that controlled the wheels. There was a brief grinding of metal on metal that made Ottilie wince, then they were stopped.

"They aren't responding to radio," Ottilie said. "I guess you open the door, wave them over, and hope they're quick about it."

"Scout, get your dogs and tuck up in that bunk out of the way," Warrior said, picking up Girl as easily as Scout scooped up Shadow and nestling her in the back of the bottom bunk on the cold, bare mattress amid the totes of half-tampered-with equipment.

"Ready," Scout said when she was settled with Girl against her side, Shadow between her legs, and a hand on each of their collars in case they got it in their heads to try to run outside into the sun.

Warrior slapped her hand on the door's control panel and it pushed out away from the wall, unsealing itself before swinging out into the overly bright world.

The sun blazing through the door was blinding, as if the whiteness of it had physical form. Warrior's top half was lost in it; Scout could only make out her legs, widely spaced as she braced herself. She rocked on her heels a bit as something collided with her, then pivoted to set a girl of about ten behind her.

Scout's fingers tightened on the dog's collars as they both started growling. The girl stumbled when Warrior released her but quickly got her footing, one hand on the top of the mini-fridge as she straightened to look into the depths of the bunk. Long, lanky, dirty blonde hair fell back from her face in neat sheets when she raised her head and icy blue eyes passed over Shadow and Girl before resting on Scout. If she was experiencing any momentary blindness after leaving the dazzling intensity of the outside world, she didn't show it. She didn't show any feeling at all, just calmly blinked as the dogs continued to growl at her presence.

Her stern face was a horrible mismatch to the bright pink outfit she was wearing, a long T-shirt with a sassy girl character from some comic winking at the world and leggings covered with hearts. Scout wondered who had dressed her, and how they had gotten this girl to allow herself to be so dressed. She didn't look like the threat of violence would move her. But what could she be bribed with?

The door slammed closed and Scout could hear the whir of motors as it pulled itself back into its recess. Warrior was holding a young woman by the arm as the woman slowly lowered her hand from her eyes to look at the interior of the rover around her. She looked familiar, but Scout couldn't quite place her. Someone from the capital, certainly, because although her flowing white blouse and loose-fitting black trousers were of a simple cut and an unadorned design, the material was of the highest quality. Highest Planet Dweller quality, that is; not so fine as what Warrior was wearing.

Shoulder-length hair of rich brown with strands of gold that flashed even in the dark interior of the rover, dark green eyes, skin a healthy tan but with no signs of past sunburns or other damage. Who was she? She seemed so familiar, and yet Scout was certain this face was much changed from the memory she was trying to match it to. She looked like she had been ill or still was ill with something chronic. Her flesh had a sickly tinge under the glow of the tan, and she looked unnaturally thin, her cheeks hollow and her eyes watery and red.

"Ah," Ottilie said in sudden insight. "You're the governor's daughter."

Scout added an "ah" of her own. That's where she'd seen this woman before, in news videos.

"Is that a fact?" Warrior asked.

The young woman hesitated, but in the end just nodded.

"Ruth Sawyer," Ottilie said with a low whistle. "Imagine finding the likes of you out here where we less social types lurk."

"Yes," Warrior said. "What an interesting coincidence."

6

EBBA WENT BACK UP to the cockpit and soon the rover was back in motion, jogging side to side as the wheels rolled in and out of ruts. Scout still held on to both of the dogs' collars. Unusually, it was Girl who was still growling low in her throat, an almost subsonic sound. Shadow stayed close to Scout's side, tipping his head as if trying to hear what was upsetting Girl. It didn't seem to be Ruth that she was growling at, but the little girl. The little girl didn't seem afraid. She just stood in the middle of the rover, hands clasped together, watching Scout and the dogs in a disinterested way.

Ebba came back down the ladder and shut the hatch to the cockpit behind her. "Bad news," she said. "The comms are down. We can't reach any of the cities. I'm sorry. I'm sure you wanted to be able to call your father and tell him you're safe."

"That's kind of you. Our comms were down as well, I guess because of the storm, but I thank you for checking," Ruth said. She wasn't meeting anyone's eyes, and Scout had a feeling she wasn't exactly upset she couldn't talk to her father.

"Who's the kid?" Ottilie asked.

"Her name is Clementine," Ruth said. "She's a foundling I've been taking care of. She doesn't speak. No one knows what happened to her family, but she's been living with my father and I for a while now."

Clementine was still staring at Scout and the dogs without even blinking. Scout didn't blame Girl for growling; the girl was giving her the creeps as well.

"So, what were you and your foundling doing out in the middle of nowhere in a town car? Were you kidnapped and taken out of the city?" Ottilie asked.

Ruth gave a nervous laugh. Her eyes moved from one of them to the other, as if hoping to find an ally. "Um," she said, then laughed again.

"I don't think we need to grill her on that," Warrior said, "not unless we all want to explain what we were doing out here."

"Well, it's not like we don't have the time," Ottilie said.

"If it's all the same to you, I'd rather not say," Ruth said, nervous laughter gone.

"State secret?" Ottilie asked.

"It doesn't matter," Warrior said. "We're all in this now. This storm is going to last for a couple of days. No need to find reasons to hate each other just yet."

"You mean reasons like the fact that she is a Space Farer?" Ruth asked, pointing to Ebba.

Scout was impressed. It'd taken her much longer to notice. But then Ruth, being the daughter of the governor, had much more experience with Space Farers.

"Yes, exactly," Warrior said. "Right now, we all have the same mission: getting through this storm alive. Ruth, we're on our way to a beacon that appears to be underground. We don't know what we'll find when we get there, but it's our best chance. Unless you know something better?"

"No," Ruth said. "I don't know of any shelters this far out from the cities."

Girl's growling slowly slid up to a higher pitch. Shadow's body was incredibly tense, and his eyes never left Clementine. "Hey, new girl," Scout said. "Can you stop staring at my dogs?"

Clementine said nothing. Ruth reached out a hand to grasp her shoulder, and she turned to look at her benefactor.

"Are you thirsty? Or maybe hungry?" Ebba asked. "We have some water and some biscuits here. Were you trapped in that town car long? It must have been stifling in there."

"We still had power to run the climate control," Ruth said.

Clementine sat down at the table and helped herself to the remains of Scout's biscuit, rapidly putting piece after piece into her mouth while staring fixedly at each of the others in turn.

"There's something unsettling about a kid who won't talk," Ottilie said.

"She's no stranger than the rest of you," Ruth said. "You two dress alike, but I can see you fought on opposite sides of the war. And you," she said, turning to Warrior, "well, you're not from around here, are you?"

Warrior shrugged.

"And what's with that kid with the dogs?" Ruth asked.

"Nothing weird about a kid having dogs," Warrior said.

"Why does that one dog not stop growling?" Ruth asked.

"She doesn't like to be stared at," Scout said, glaring at Clementine, who was, in fact, once more staring at the dogs even as she kept shoveling biscuit into her mouth. "Have you been starving her?"

"Of course not," Ruth said. "She's had a hard childhood. Like I said, we found her on the streets. She couldn't talk, she had no one to take care of her, and she was eating whatever she could find. I don't need to tell you, that wasn't much. I think she's still trying to catch back up."

Scout glared back at Clementine. She had little sympathy. She had been on her own without anyone to take care of her since she was younger than Clementine, and she never had a rich benefactor. She was thin, but not as thin as other kids who lived on the streets. Scout knew many kids in much worse shape, kids who didn't go around glaring at people.

Scout felt someone else looking at her and glanced over at Warrior. It was hard to tell with the reflective lenses, but Scout felt like she was being chastised. She supposed she was being judgy, and maybe that was unfair.

But then why was Girl still growling? She touched the back of the dog's neck, leaning forward to whisper comforting words into her ear. After a moment, Girl finally stopped growling, flopping down between Scout's legs but keeping her chin on Scout's knee so she could keep watching the new girl.

"So," Ottilie said with exaggerated casualness. "Your daddy has had quite a lot to say recently. Likes to talk big, doesn't he?" Scout didn't know what she was referring to, but then Scout tuned out most political talk. In truth, any of it that didn't mention the rebels, she just let flow past her.

"It's complicated," Ruth said shortly.

"But you can't say it's not our business," Ottilie said. "You're stirring up a political shit storm. We're all going to get swept up in it."

"I think I know a little bit more about that than you do," Ruth said.

"About war? I don't think so," Ottilie scoffed. "Because war? That's where this whole mess is going to end."

"What are you worried about?" Ruth asked. "You're too old to be conscripted again."

Ottilie's hands curled into fists, but Ebba put her own hand on Ottilie's forearm and left it there until she relaxed them.

"Since we're all trapped together inside this box," Warrior said, "perhaps we should keep our conversation to neutral matters like the weather."

"Oh, the weather," Ottilie said with a sharp laugh. "On this planet, nothing is more political than the weather."

Warrior clicked her tongue against the inside of her teeth. "Okay, I'll give. How is the weather political?"

"Not so much the weather," Ebba said, "but storms like this one."

"Oh," Scout said, as the meaning dawned on her.

"Explain, Scout," Warrior said.

"The magnetic shield that's supposed to protect us from solar flares —it's generated by satellites. Satellites in space," Scout said. "Space, where Planet Dwellers never go. Where the Space Farers control everything."

"I see," Warrior said. "Yes, that does sound political."

"It's obviously more complicated than that," Ruth said.

"Obviously," Warrior said. "It always is."

The rocking back and forth of the rover slowed to a stop, and the engine cut off. Ebba turned and opened the hatch to the cockpit, Ottilie and Warrior following close behind as she climbed back up in the driver's seat. "We're there," Ebba said, "but I don't see a thing."

She and Ottilie looked at all the panels while Warrior looked through the narrow band of windows, slowly turning in a circle. Scout really wished there were other windows in the rover so she could see out as well. Ruth slid onto the bench across from Clementine, her back to Scout. Scout wondered what her story was. It'd been a few days since she'd been in a city for more than a minute, which wasn't long enough to hear any news. Why would the governor's daughter go missing? How had she ended up out in the middle of nowhere alone with her ward?

"There," Warrior said, pointing through one of the windows. "Do you see? There's a little hill, and something in the side of the hill. See it?"

"I'll pull up closer," Ebba said, bringing the engines back to life. She made little nudges on the controls, and the rover rolled slowly forward. Then they stopped once more.

"Nice work," Warrior said. "You lined that up perfectly with the door."

"Lined what up?" Scout asked as Warrior came back down the ladder.

"Hard to say," Warrior said. "Help me get into this suit."

"You only have two suits," Ruth noted.

"It'll be enough," Warrior said. "I'm going out alone first, to see what's out there."

"You're leaving us?" Ruth asked.

"Of course not," Warrior said. "In fact, I'll be in contact with Scout the entire time."

"You will?" Scout said.

"Yes," Warrior said, taking something else off her belt and pressing it into Scout's hands.

"What's this?" Scout asked. It looked like a pair of glasses, only when she put them on she couldn't see a thing.

"I'll activate the link in a minute," Warrior said as she pulled the suit up over her arms. "You'll see what I see, and you'll hear what I say. And vice versa."

"I was hoping for an opening big enough to just drive the rover right inside," Ottilie said.

"Yeah, me too," Warrior said, zipping the suit up and reaching for the helmet. "It seemed logical, with the beacon and all. But it's been a few years. Sometimes things get buried by time."

"And if there's nothing here but a beacon?" Ottilie asked.

"We can worry about that when I get back," Warrior said. "Step back from the door. The storm is more intense than before. I'll be quick. Be prepared to seal this after me very quickly."

"How are we going to get out of here one by one with the other suit? The last person to go is going to already be baked by all this opening and closing of the door," Ruth said.

"One thing at a time," Warrior said, then signaled for Ottilie and Ebba to help her. They opened the door just enough for her to slip outside, then slammed it shut behind her.

"Easy for her to say," Ruth said bitterly. "She's the one who is going to be wearing a suit the entire time, not us. And look at her. She probably has implants or nanites or something—none of this even hurts her."

"Don't be ridiculous," Scout said. "If that were true, she wouldn't be using a suit." Although she too wondered. There was just something about Warrior that made you doubt she was entirely human.

"Can you see anything?" Ottilie asked.

Scout dropped the glasses back down over her eyes, keeping one arm around each dog. She didn't like being blind to the room she was in, but she was scarcely going to turn down the trust that Warrior had just put in her. For a moment, her vision was still black, then there was a crackling sound in her ears and a blinding light in her eyes.

"Aah!" Scout cried, but fought the urge to rip the glasses off her face.

"Sorry about that," Warrior said. "It's a bit brighter out here than inside the rover."

"It must be nearly noon," Scout said.

"You're getting my raw data feed," Warrior said. "Sorry, I can't adjust that."

"This isn't what you see?"

"I have some filters in place."

"To adjust for the sun?"

"Among other things. For instance, someone is out here with me."

"I don't see anything," Scout said. Her eyes were adjusting to the bright light, but there was nothing around but dirt and scrubby grass. They had left the grain fields behind and were really out in the sticks now. She saw a small hill that Warrior was walking towards, only a few steps away, but no sign of a person.

"There's an opening in the hill," Warrior said.

"Where?"

"It's quite small."

Scout's stomach gave a sickening lurch as Warrior suddenly dropped to the ground and began crawling forward. Scout saw Warrior's gloved hands moving over reddish dirt as the dazzling brightness of the day gave way to the murky darkness of the hole she was crawling into.

"Are you sure this is a good idea?" Scout asked. "You just said there was a person in there. How do you know they're friendly?"

"Like I said, kid. We're on the same mission here."

"Surviving the storm," Scout said.

"Exactly."

"What does she see?" Ottilie asked in a harsh whisper.

"Nothing yet," Scout said. She was looking at darkness, but it was darkness with a certain pattern to it. When Warrior got back to her feet, Scout could tell by the way the darkness swirled down.

Then she was blinded again, but not by warm sunlight. This was a cold, artificial light. And someone was shining it deliberately right into Warrior's eyes.

7

SCOUT HAD to shut her eyes against the onslaught of that light. She wondered what Warrior with her filtered vision could see. She waited for something to happen, for Warrior to move or speak or for the person down in that hole with her to do something, but she heard nothing. She buried a hand in each of the dogs' fur, that comforting gesture grounding her inside the rover she could no longer see.

"Warrior?" she whispered when her patience at last gave out.

"Hey, friend," Warrior said, not to her.

"Not sure you're my friend," someone said. The voice sounded distant in Scout's ear, not as close as Warrior, but still clear. It was a hard voice, but it had the same rich vowels of the Planet Dweller elite as Ruth spoke with.

"Well, I'm not your enemy," Warrior said. "You're trying to get into that door? I want to get into that door too."

"Just looking for shelter from the storm?" the new woman asked, an edge of sarcasm to her voice.

"Exactly. So why don't you lower your light."

The light dropped away and Scout could finally see. The tunnel Warrior had crawled through had opened into a slightly larger space, still not big enough to fit a rover, but big enough to fit the six of them plus the two dogs plus this new woman. The walls were the same red dirt Warrior had just crawled through, and the open space was narrow but twisted in a gradual arc, widening at about shoulder level, then closing up again. A few scraggly grass roots hung down from the low ceiling, dried out and dead-looking.

But at the back of the space was a metal wall, and in the center of the wall was a door. Scout guessed this was the entrance to something hidden deeper underground, some building meant to be topside, no bigger than an outhouse, that had over the years been buried by the blowing red dirt, packed down by hard rains and baked in the sun. It brought to mind movies she had seen from Old Earth, lost civilizations rediscovered after endless centuries, only no one had been on this planet earlier than a dozen decades ago. And even if it was some long-lost structure, what was this woman doing here?

Warrior was walking toward the woman, but slowly, giving Scout lots of time to look her over. She was in a hover chair, an expensive model, all sleek curves of chrome if a bit scuffed and dirty, much like the woman. She was dressed like Ruth in a certain careless elegance, her long black hair pulled back and tied tight at her nape, the end pulled forward to drape over one shoulder. The style was reminiscent of Ebba's, but she definitely wasn't a Space Farer, not with that healthy glow to her rich brown skin. She would have looked like a prosperous Planet Dweller businesswoman if not for the red dirt all over her. Her hands were caked with it, a few of her carefully manicured nails broken, and she had long streaks of dirt down her front.

There was no way to ride a hover chair into this space, not even her model built like a pod that curved around the front up to her waist. She must be sitting cross-legged under the curving panel, if she had legs at all. She must have barely gotten the chair through the tunnel by sending it through empty, then programming it to make the journey on its own as she pulled herself down after it.

But how had she gotten out here in the first place?

"I can help with that," Warrior said, nodding to the pry bar the woman had left wedged between door and doorframe before Warrior had interrupted her. The area of the door and frame around the bar had many deep scratches, as if it'd taken her many tries to find purchase. "I think I'd have more leverage."

"I'm stronger than I look," the woman said.

"I don't doubt that," Warrior said, "but you're trying to force the locking mechanism halfway up the door. It's a little awkward to do from your chair."

"What's happening?" Ottilie hissed at Scout.

"There is a door, and a woman trying to open the door, a woman in a hover chair," Scout reported.

"A hover chair," Ottilie repeated. "Here. Beyond the edge of civilization. In a hover chair."

"Well, yeah," Scout said. "She only looks a little bit younger than you. Maybe she was hurt in the war?"

"Many were," Ebba said, "but the wounded from both sides, the badly wounded, the paralyzed, they all went up into space."

"Maybe not all," Scout said. "Surely it wasn't mandatory."

"Scout," Warrior said, her voice only slightly showing the strain as she pushed on the pry bar.

"Yes?"

"Get the little girl in the suit first. Send her out to me. She'll find the hole in the hill. It's going to take a while to get this door open, and we need to get you all in faster than that."

"Got it." Scout pushed the glasses back on top of her head. "She wants us to come to her. She said send the girl first."

"And then what?" Ottilie asked.

"I'll send her back with my suit," Warrior said, as if she could hear what they were saying. "Each of you will come, take a suit back, then come back to the hole and take your suit off for the next person. Sound like a plan?"

"Got it," Scout said, then repeated it to the others.

Ebba and Ottilie helped Clementine into the suit, using a belt to pull up the extra fabric so she wouldn't trip.

"Straight out from the door, you'll find a little hill, and there's a hole in the ground at the bottom of the hill. Climb into the hole," Scout said.

Clementine nodded. Then Ebba and Ottilie opened the door just long enough to push her outside.

"Ruth, you're next," Scout said. "Then either of you two. I'll go last."

She was afraid they were going to ask her why, but they just nodded gravely. Perhaps they guessed. Scout hugged her dogs tighter. Now that Clementine had gone, they were both in much better spirits. Girl thumped her tail loudly against the wall of the rover, and Shadow licked at her chin.

"We should pack," Ebba said, and Ottilie nodded. Ebba pulled two enormous bags from the same cabinet she had stored the suits in and she and Ottilie went to the kitchenette and started emptying their food stores into the two bags.

Scout dropped the glasses back down over her eyes, but there wasn't much to see. Warrior was leaning over the pry bar, pushing with all her might. The woman in the hover chair was at the corner of her field of vision, hands clasped nervously as she watched Warrior work.

"I don't suppose you asked where she came from?" Scout asked.

"You suppose correctly," Warrior said. "Plenty of time for questions... once we're on the other side of this door." She had taken off the suit before starting on the pry bar, and it was lying on the ground near the woman in the hover chair. Scout could just see as Clementine emerged from the tunnel, snatched up the suit, and disappeared out of Warrior's vision again.

"She's coming," she said to the others. A moment later, there was a muffled knock at the door, and Ebba and Ottilie pushed it open just long enough to pull her inside.

"Did you get a name anyway?" Scout asked.

Warrior made a sound somewhere between a groan and a chuckle. "So, got a name?"

"Oh, are you talking to me this time?" the woman in the hover chair asked primly.

"Yeah," Warrior asked before leaning back into the pry bar.

"Call me Liv."

"Pleased to meet you, Liv," Warrior said, the last few words lost in a loud grunt as she strained at the bar.

"I'll reserve judgment before saying the same," Liv said.

"Suit yourself," Warrior said.

"Ready," Ruth said, and Scout lifted the glasses to watch Ruth and Clementine disappear into the light.

"How much are we being exposed to?" Ebba asked Ottilie in a low voice.

"Does it matter?" Ottilie asked offhandedly, but then added, "A lot. Maybe too much for the little ones."

"If the beacon is part of an original colonial shelter, they might have radiation meds."

"Still? And would they still be any good?"

Scout tried to tune them out. They weren't saying anything she hadn't already been thinking, only she wasn't so much worried about herself.

Ruth returned with Clementine's suit and waited for Ebba to put it on. Warrior didn't seem to be making any progress, but her strength wasn't flagging yet either. Scout heard Ebba's grunt as she slung one of the overloaded bags over her shoulder, then the clang as the door was shut behind her.

"Do you have any explosives in here?" Scout lifted her glasses to ask Ottilie. "Something small, like a mining charge, to blow the door?"

"I don't think so," Ottilie said, but then her face lit up and she turned to look at the mess around the table. There wasn't much else to do while she waited for Ebba to return with Ruth's suit. She was engrossed in digging through a tote when Ebba knocked, so Scout got off the bunk to push open the door.

"I just need a second," Ottilie said, gathering what seemed like far too many bits of junk into her bag.

"Oh, I've got it," Ebba said. "Get dressed. I'll get your bag ready."

"You know what I'm thinking?"

"Of course I do, dear," Ebba said, the fondness clear even through the speakers in Scout's helmet.

"I'll be back for you next," Ottilie said to Scout, who just gave a nod. She didn't trust herself to speak.

Scout folded up the glasses and put them in her shirt pocket, then leaned down to gather Shadow close in her arms, sparing a hand to touch Girl's head. It seemed to take a lot longer for Ottilie to return. Perhaps that was a kindness.

Finally, there was a knock at the door, brisk and forceful, and she pushed it open, but when the suited figure turned and removed her helmet, it was Warrior standing in front of her.

"Ottilie had an idea," Scout guessed.

"Well, I wasn't having much luck, so I said I'd come back for you and give her a shot at opening the door." She handed Scout the spare suit and Scout slowly began to put it on.

Then Warrior took off her own suit.

"What are you doing?"

"What does it look like?" Warrior asked.

"You can't stay here."

"Why would I do that? It's not far from here to the hole. I'll be fine. I won't go into the specifics on that, but you can trust me. I can take it. Your dogs, on the other hand…"

Scout felt tears spring to her eyes but blinked them back hard. She felt compelled to point out, "Just one of them is mine. Technically."

"Technically," Warrior said, the corner of her mouth quirking again. "No one gets left behind, kid. But you're going to have to help me get them inside. I don't think they're going to understand or enjoy what's about to happen to them."

"True enough," Scout said. Girl went into the bottom of the suit amiably enough, but Shadow had no desire to be thrust inside on top of her. Scout had to stop trying to be gentle and just hold him down until everything was zipped up and sealed. Then Warrior tied the arms and legs together to make a sling that crossed her body.

"I'll go first, since I'm going to want to run. You follow after."

"Got it," Scout said.

The door was opened to the noonday light once more, although the suit's helmet instantly adjusted and Scout could see clearly. She stood transfixed for a moment. The sky above her was crisscrossed with streaks, fading away as quickly as they formed, but new ones always forming everywhere. She had never seen so many. It was like the sky was made of eggshell, a rapidly shattering eggshell.

When she looked down again, she found that Warrior and the dogs had already crawled down the tunnel to the space below. How long had she been standing there, just gaping at the sky? Scout dropped down to her hands and knees to follow. When she got to the end of the tunnel, she started to get to her feet. She heard a clamor of voices, but only dimly, and she realized her helmet's external mic was off.

Still on one knee, she heard a faint boom and looked up to see a wall of sand rushing toward her. Then she was blasted backwards, hitting the packed dirt over the tunnel entrance and tumbling to the ground.  .

8

SCOUT WAS SPRAWLED out flat on her back, watching the dirt settle around her as she fought to catch her breath. Someone was shining Liv's light around, making the dust motes flash like stars. Or was Scout just thinking she saw stars? They danced around her, sparkling as they swooped along air currents that cycloned around the room, unable to find an escape. How badly had she hit her head? She tried not to remember the day she'd been blown off her bike. She had taken much more of a tumble that day. Surely she wasn't seriously hurt now, but she was reluctant to try moving too soon. Then faces clustered around her and hands reached for the seal of her helmet.

"Did you break anything?" Ottilie asked, sounding annoyed.

Scout, still not able to draw a proper breath, just shook her head.

"I thought you were right behind me," Warrior said.

"You would've had time to get to cover if you'd been right behind her," Ottilie said.

"…'m okay," Scout said, struggling to get up on her elbows.

"Are you sure?" Warrior asked.

Scout nodded. "How are the dogs?" she asked.

"I suppose I should let them out," Warrior said, setting the helmet down and disappearing in the clouds of dust.

"You blew the door?" she asked Ottilie.

"On the first try."

"What's on the other side?" Scout asked.

"Get up and let's go see," Ottilie said. She extended a hand and Scout took it, letting herself be pulled to her feet. She was sore all over, but not really hurt. Liv, in her hover chair, had already moved closer to the doorway and was shining her light within, but beyond was only darkness.

"It goes down," Liv said. "I can't tell how far."

"Down is good," Ebba said. "Down is safer."

"You were already here," Scout said to Liv. "Do you know what this place is?"

"I followed the beacon, same as you," Liv said, waving her hand over a display panel built into the arm of her hover chair, a map with a flashing light in the center.

"That's a nice chair," Scout said, bending to examine the small panels and controls clustered on both chair arms.

"It's one of the newer models," Ruth said. "Very expensive. Rare."

"I was on a waiting list," Liv said. "My last chair was far more rudimentary." She slapped one of her rock-hard biceps to be sure they knew just how rudimentary she meant.

"You must work for the government if you got on that list," Ruth said, narrowing her eyes as if squinting at Liv's face might make it more familiar to her.

Then Shadow gave a joyous bark as Warrior let him out of the suit. He charged over to jump on Scout and she bent to take his head in both her hands and rub his ears the way he liked. Girl soon joined them, calmer but with her tail wagging hard enough to thump loudly against the wall of the cavern, sending more clouds of dust into the already thick air.

"What else is in your bag?" Ruth asked Ebba.

"Freeze-dried food," Ebba said. "I couldn't bring any water—I didn't have a large enough container for carrying it—but I guess we can go back if we need to."

"There must've been something," Ruth said. "We're going to need water more than we'll need food."

"Ebba is right," Warrior said. "We can always go back, but for now, we should explore this tunnel. It's possible we won't even need the rover's water." She folded up the spare suit and handed it to Ebba, who tucked it into her bag. "Shall we?"

"Maybe Scout should go first. Her and the dogs," Ottilie said.

Scout wasn't afraid of caves or the dark or the unknown, and neither was Shadow. They had poked through many a hidey-hole together while waiting out storms or midday heat up in the hills. This wasn't so different.

And there was always the chance that this was another rebel hideout. Maybe this was the day she would finally meet them face-to-face.

"Scout and I will lead with the dogs," Warrior said. "Ruth, you come behind a bit with Clementine. Ottilie and Ebba, you bring up the rear. Keep an eye on our six, no reason not to be cautious. Liv, where should we put you?"

"I can take care of myself," she said, drawing herself up taller in her hover chair.

"No doubt," Warrior said. "You got out here somehow. I didn't see another vehicle out there, and I could see for kilometers. I'm not asking for an explanation, just making an observation."

"I'll stay in the middle, with the little one," Liv said, looking at the ever-silent Clementine. Clementine was standing close to Ruth, half using Ruth as a shield, as everyone was suddenly looking at her. But there was no fear or shyness in her eyes.

Scout called the dogs to her as Warrior pushed the dangling door a little further open. Shadow trotted on ahead, not bothered by the dark, but Girl stayed close to Scout's side. Warrior took a light of her own off her belt and shone it down the tunnel. It wasn't as bright as Liv's, but it would do.

The cyclone of red dirt formed by the explosion in the arc-shaped cavern had bounced back through the now-open door. Some of the red dirt had settled to the floor, but some still hung in the air. Stone floor, stone walls, stone ceiling, all squared off in the telltale signs of the colonizers' mining machines. Shadow walked at the very edge of Warrior's light, looking back from time to time to make sure they were all still following him. They walked in silence, the only sounds the echoes of their footfalls and the soft hum from Liv's hover chair.

Suddenly Shadow charged ahead, and Girl ran after him.

"Dogs!" Scout started to yell, but Warrior put a hand on her arm and shook her head.

"There could be trouble," Scout said in a hissing whisper.

"Yes, and I don't want to run into it. Trust their instincts; they'll retreat if they need to," Warrior said. She brushed the edges of her shirt back from her hips, but didn't draw her gun. She did quicken her pace, though, and Scout did as well. She could hear the dogs in the darkness ahead, the snuffle of their breath as they followed scent trails, the click of their nails as they broke into another run.

Then something crashed, as if one of the dogs had knocked several things over at once, followed by a string of human curses. There was another crash, then a smaller one, more like a thrown object, and one of the dogs yelped. Again, Warrior put a restraining hand on Scout's arm to keep her from rushing ahead.

"I know somebody's there," the curser said. "Those dogs didn't let themselves in."

"You're right," Warrior said, and at the edge of her light they could see the tunnel end in a steep flight of stairs spiraling down. There was no sign of the dogs. "Don't be startled. We're just travelers in need of a place to wait out the storm."

"Find another place," the woman yelled back. "Mine's not open."

Warrior, keeping her hands near her hips but in a nonobvious way, went first down the stairs. "If you live here, you well know there is no other place."

"Not my problem. I'm not looking for company."

Scout followed Warrior down the stairs. The stairs made a complete circle as they descended, and Warrior's form became a silhouette as the light from her flashlight was swallowed up by a brighter light coming from the bottom of the stairs. Warrior switched off her light and put it back on her belt.

"I'm sure we can come to some sort of arrangement for the inconvenience," Warrior said as she walked into the light.

Scout glanced back at the others, who had stopped halfway down the stairs. Ruth pulled Clementine closer to her. Ebba was holding her bag open to let Ottilie quietly dig through it. Ottilie was engrossed, but Ebba raised her chin at Scout, then tipped her head to suggest she should keep going down the tunnel. Scout nodded back. Perhaps it would be best not to all go in at once, not if this woman was as jumpy as she sounded. But *she* had to go; she had to find her dogs.

Slowly, she followed the last turn.

All she could see was the silhouette of Warrior, hands near her hips but not awkwardly so, standing several meters from Scout. Small, flat silver packages were scattered across the floor at Warrior's feet: food rations, likely as old as this station.

"I'm not interested in an arrangement," the still-unseen woman said. "That's close enough."

"We can't wait out the storm in the tunnel, we don't have enough water," Warrior said, still stepping forward into the light.

"Like I said, not my problem."

Scout crept after Warrior, pausing to look down at the packages on the floor. Definitely food rations; she could see labels that read BEEF STROGANOFF and CHICKEN À LA KING.

"Who's lurking behind you?" the woman demanded, the beginnings of panic edging into her voice.

"Just my friend, Scout. She's harmless."

"But you're not?"

Warrior gave a little shrug. Scout took a few more steps past the spill of rations, stepping around the overturned crate they had fallen from, and out of the narrow tunnel into a larger space. The light was intensely bright, but it was coming from a single source in the center of the room's ceiling. Scout shaded her eyes first with her hand and then with the brim of her hat.

A woman of impressive girth stood with her feet planted wide apart, a rifle aimed at Warrior. Her dark skin had a grayish hue to it, as if she didn't often get out into the sun. Her hair was a frizzy white cloud that floated all around her head. Her back was up against a table long enough to seat a dozen. A bottle of something amber-colored was near her elbow, a ring of condensate still marring the plastic tabletop molded to look like wood, but the glass that should be resting there was missing.

"It's just the two of you?" the woman asked, the end of her rifle wavering a bit.

"And the dogs," Warrior said.

"I don't like dogs," she said in a low growl and groped for her missing glass. When she couldn't find it, she chanced a look back, swore under her breath, and took a swift pull from the bottle.

"And also five others," Warrior said.

The woman sputtered as some of her drink went down the wrong pipe, but kept the rifle up. "No. Too many."

"Don't be silly. Look at this place."

She lifted her hands slightly, palms up, and Scout took her eyes off the woman to look around the room. It had an octagonal shape, the walls ahead and to the left and right, each with a doorway in the center leading into darkness. The walls all around those doorways were covered in shelving, each shelf crammed to the max with crates and sacks of unknown contents, open tubs filled with hardware and small electronics, or tightly wrapped coils of rope. There was a generous blanket of dust over nearly everything, even the table and chairs in the center of the room under the light—everything except the area around one of the chairs where the woman now stood, and where her bottle waited for her.

"Are you alone?" Scout asked. "So much space. How many more rooms?" She started to head to another doorway to see what lay beyond, but the woman moved her rifle from Warrior to Scout and Warrior put out a hand, motioning for Scout to stop moving.

"This storm is going to last for four days," Warrior said to the woman.

"I know. I have equipment," she said testily.

"We don't have to get in your hair," Warrior went on. "As long as we can have access to water and perhaps some sanitary facilities, we can otherwise keep to ourselves."

"You'll be stealing my stuff," she said.

"Why would we want it? This stuff is ancient," Scout said.

"Have some respect," the woman said.

"We won't touch your things," Warrior said. "I will personally guarantee that. I will keep the others in line."

The woman lowered the rifle about halfway and bit her lip as she thought. Scout stood where Warrior had told her to stop moving, halfway between the doorway to the tunnel and the doorway to something else, something she couldn't quite see, but she thought she heard a soft hum, like from a refrigeration unit. Could there be jolo here?

The woman dropped the rifle to her side with a sigh. "I don't suppose there's much point in arguing. You have me outnumbered anyway, and I don't intend to spend the next four days living under siege, fighting off looters." She reached behind her and switched off the spotlight. Scout blinked for a moment or two before the now-dimmer room came back into focus.

"Thank you," Warrior said. "I'm Warrior. This is Scout."

"Viola," the woman said and reached for her bottle again. She had it to her lips and was about to take another swallow when a long howl echoed from one of the darkened doorways and her gray complexion went even paler.

"Tubbins!" she said.

"Who's Tubbins?" Warrior asked, but Scout was afraid she already knew the answer to that question.

The skitter of dog claws across the stone floor grew louder, then Shadow came charging back into the room, running to Scout's side. Girl lumbered after, encumbered by something in her mouth—an orange and white something curled in a tight ball, its back end clenched far too tightly in Girl's massively strong jaws.

She dropped it at Scout's feet and moved back a bit to sit with her tail thumping loudly against the floor.

The thing whimpered, then lifted its head to look up at Scout with imploring eyes. It tried to pull itself toward her, away from the still-tail-wagging Girl, but its back end dragged uselessly behind it.

"Tubbins!" Viola shrieked, and before Scout even realized she had raised it again, the sound of the rifle discharging rent the air.

# 9

SCOUT HAD NEVER BEEN SO close to a firing weapon before. Under the octagonal room's cavernous ceiling, the echoing noise was painfully loud. Scout flinched, her whole body contracting into itself and her eyes closing. She stayed like that as the echoes died away. The plasma bolt must have struck somewhere quite close to her, the ozone filling her sinuses.

The silence after the echoes faded was worse. She knew she hadn't been shot, but she was afraid to open her eyes to look at her dogs. Shadow must be okay; he had been close beside her, and she was unharmed.

And it had been Girl who had crushed Tubbins. Why had she done that? Such cruelty—was she really capable of that? She with her big eyes and dopey manner. She and Shadow had chased many a critter through the grain fields and had, she suspected, eaten more than a few when the pair were gone from her sight for too long. But a cat—surely a cat was a different thing? How could Girl not know the difference between prey and pet?

All those nights with Shadow curled up against her belly, Girl had flopped down to sleep with her head on Scout's ankle. She had been sleeping with a killer, a remorseless and cruel killer.

Then she heard Viola swearing again and finally opened her eyes. Shadow was still standing close to her calf, and Girl still sat hovering over the cat, although she had stopped wagging her tail and looked nervous.

"No deal. I want all of you out of here," Viola said. Her rifle was on the floor at her feet and she was massaging one wrist as she glared at Warrior.

"No need to be hasty," Warrior said. "I can help your cat. Tubbins. But I'm going to need you to put that rifle away."

"Why?" Viola asked, barking out a laugh. "What did you do to me?"

Scout was wondering the same thing. Viola kept massaging her wrist and glaring at Warrior. What had Warrior done to make her drop her rifle? And who had she been trying to shoot?

"All the same," Warrior said, "I'd feel better if that rifle were put away."

"So would we," Ottilie said. She was at the doorway to the tunnel, standing amid the scattered ration packets. She clutched something in her hand, something she kept out of sight. Ebba was close behind her, as were the others.

"I don't want you people here," Viola said, but she seemed to find Warrior's reflective lenses fixed on her just as unsettling as Scout did. She stopped massaging her wrist and picked up her rifle, holding it in the middle, nowhere near the trigger. She carried it across the room to where there was a sort of bar in front of one of the shelves. The bar was also of plastic molded to look like wood. When it was new, it might have been more convincing, but the scratches and dings of long use were definitely not the splintering of wood. The chairs at the table and the tall stools at the bar were the usual cold, practical metal: no adornments, just the few spare lines it took to define a chair. They at least weren't showing their age.

Viola stepped onto the bottom shelf, not tall enough to reach the top shelf on her own, and put the rifle up high inside a case with a palm lock. There was a clanking of glass as she dug around behind the bar, then she returned to the table, another glass in hand.

"Scout, bring the cat here," Warrior said. The cat was still looking up at Scout with imploring eyes. Scout bent to pick up the cat, and Girl surged forward as if trying to take her prize back.

"No!" Scout said as she cuddled the cat close to her chest. Girl looked confused at her anger but still tried to catch the end of the cat's tail. "No! Bad girl!"

"Dogs are a menace," Viola said bitterly as she poured some of the amber liquid into the glass. Her eyes dropped as Scout, with the cat in her arms, drew nearer. Scout didn't blame her for not wanting to look. The cat was half-flattened; it was a gruesome sight.

"That one's not my dog. Not really," Scout said. "The well-behaved one is my dog."

"They both came in here with you. That's all I know," Viola said, taking a drink.

"Scout." There was an edge to Warrior's voice, and Scout hurried to bring the cat to where Warrior was waiting at the bar.

"How can you fix this?" Scout asked as Warrior ran her hands gently over the cat's body.

"It's costly," Warrior said. "Too much for a cat, really. But your dogs just made a hard situation harder." She lifted her face and pinned Scout down with those blank lenses. Scout fought the urge to squirm.

"It's not really my fault," Scout said.

"It's your responsibility," Warrior said. "You may not have chosen that dog, but she chose you. She's yours. She's your responsibility, and you've been neglecting her. You do her a disservice not to train her as well as your other dog."

"She's not that bright," Scout said.

Warrior just looked at her until Scout dropped her head. She didn't want to say out loud that Warrior was probably right. Training Shadow had been something she had done with her father, and every time she tried to teach Girl something, it made her sad. She remembered how patient her father had been, how her little brother had squealed and clapped his hands when Shadow had done his tricks, like playing dead or walking on his hind feet. Of course, those weren't the kinds of things to teach Girl, but still.

Trying to do it on her own only reminded her of everything she had lost.

Warrior had finished examining the cat but was lost in thought, stroking the cat's head as she considered what to do.

"You can't fix it," Scout said. "Her pelvis is crushed. Too many little pieces—we can't set that."

"You're not wrong about that," Warrior said. "But there is something I can do." She pulled a tiny blade from her belt and held it over her spread palm. She seemed to be concentrating on something, just staring at her hand. Then Scout saw something wiggle, something under Warrior's skin. Warrior put the point of the blade under her skin, digging in to get under the wiggling thing. Her blood welled up, but thickly, slowly. Her blood was dark, more purple than red even when exposed to air. Scout saw a small metallic flash, something resting on the point of the blade. Before she got a good look at it, Warrior had stabbed it into the cat's thigh.

"What the hell are you doing?" Viola shouted as the cat shrieked, and she ran to her pet's side.

"What needs to be done," Warrior said. "I just put a nanite inside of Tubbins here. It's going to get to work helping your cat heal. It's going to take a few hours, but he'll be fine."

"Nanite," Viola repeated.

Warrior rummaged under the bar until she found a towel, cleaned her blade, and then wrapped the towel around her hand. She put the knife away and stroked the cat one more time.

The others had come into the room now, Girl once more growling low in her throat at the sight of Clementine. Ruth took Clementine by the arm, steering her further away from the dogs to the far end of the table. Ottilie set her and Ebba's sacks on the table as Ebba bent to pick up the spilled ration packets. Whatever she had been concealing in her hand was gone now.

Liv's chair floated silently to the head of the table and settled to the ground. Liv sat back, hands folded over her stomach as her eyes swept across them all.

"How many rooms are there in this place?" she asked Viola.

"Why do you want to know?" Viola asked, refusing to leave her cat's side.

"We might want to divide up into groups for safety," she said.

"No, we stick together," Warrior said.

"You know, I'm a latecomer to this little party, so I'm not entirely sure why you're in charge," Liv said coldly.

"Yeah, you have been giving a lot of orders," Ottilie said. "I'm not sure I'm cool with that, either."

"I got us all here, out of the storm," Warrior said.

"I found my own way here," Liv said.

"And I blew the door," Ottilie said.

"I'm not giving orders, I'm pointing out common sense," Warrior said. She pulled the towel back from her palm, saw that the bleeding had stopped, and tossed the towel aside, reaching for something else on her belt. She grabbed Scout's wrist and pressed the device to her forearm, triggering it. There was a hiss and a flash of pain.

"Ow!" Scout said, pulling her arm tight against her stomach.

"What is that?" Viola asked, sounding more curious than anything.

"Just a little something to fight the effects of exposure to a coronal mass ejection event. I'm guessing you don't need any," Warrior said.

"No, I've been underground the entire time," Viola said, her eyes sweeping over the other gadgets on Warrior's belt. Tubbins made a sleepy whimpering sound, and she turned her attention back to the cat.

"Surely, even if we can't agree on a leader, we can agree that we're a team," Ebba said, stacking the ration packets at the end of the table. She paused in her work to let Warrior inject her.

"We're not a team," Ruth said. "Not with you."

"Why not her in particular?" Viola asked.

"Because of this," Ruth said, reaching across the table to catch Ebba by the wrist. Warrior had pushed back her sleeve to inject into bare skin and Ruth had stopped Ebba before she could smooth her cuff back into place. They all saw the tattoo.

Viola appeared mildly surprised, but the look of cold loathing that passed over Liv's face chilled Scout to the bone. Liv quickly mimicked Viola's expression, but Scout knew she hadn't imagined it.

For whatever reason, Liv hated Space Farers, was repulsed by them. But had there also been the slightest tinge of fear?

10

SCOUT HAD ALREADY SEEN the tattoo. Warrior certainly knew of its existence whether or not she'd ever actually acknowledged it. It didn't seem like it meant much to Clementine. But Viola and Liv recoiled as if it were a loaded weapon aimed at them.

"I vote we put her back outside," Viola said. "Do you know how many of my friends and family you killed?"

"No, I don't," Ebba said, breaking Ruth's hold on her wrist with a sharp, twisting movement. Ruth hissed in pain and clutched her hand close to her chest with her other hand. Ebba may be old and long retired from the military, but clearly she was not frail or one to be bullied.

"The war is over," Ottilie said, holding out her own arm for Warrior to inject. "Nothing to be gained by rehashing all that here."

"What do you know about it?" Ruth demanded.

"Ebba was in communications," Ottilie said. "There's no blood on her hands. But mine?" She planted one fist on the table, flexing her biceps until they were all looking at her tattoo. "I know there's blood on my hands. But it's in the past."

"Nothing is ever in the past," Ruth said. "Everything about our lives today, everything is based on a foundation from yesterday. We can't ignore that."

"For the next four days you're going to," Warrior said, injecting first Ruth, then Clementine. The little girl didn't even flinch. "We're all going to be miserable enough without finding causes for squabbles."

"Is she a Space Farer too?" Viola asked Liv in a low voice. Or tried to; she had drained enough glasses of amber liquid that her low voice wasn't all that low anymore, especially pitched to carry halfway across the room.

"No, I'm not a Space Farer," Warrior said before anyone else could speak. "I'm not from here."

"Then where are you from?" Liv asked.

"I'm from a place a little nearer the galactic center," Warrior said.

"And?" Liv prompted. Viola had set her glass down, arms folded as she waited to hear the answer. Ebba and Ottilie turned to look at Warrior as well. Only Clementine seemed uninterested, her gaze focused on her hands as her fingertips traced something on the tabletop.

"And I'm a galactic marshal," Warrior finally admitted. "That's not really anything that concerns any of you."

"You have no jurisdiction here," Ottilie said.

"True," Warrior said.

"So why are you here?" Ottilie persisted.

"I'm tracking down a fugitive from justice," Warrior said.

They all looked at each other nervously.

"Not one of you. Honestly, I just got caught out in the storm like the rest of you."

"So that's why you're so bossy," Ottilie said, nodding to herself.

Warrior just shrugged. "Do you want a dose?" she asked Liv, who rolled back one silken sleeve and raised her arm with an air of quiet dignity.

"Can I have some of that?" Liv asked Viola as she rolled her sleeve back down.

Viola bit her lip as she looked at her bottle, but in the end just gave a curt nod. Liv lifted the hem of her shirt as if to clean off the mouth of the bottle, saw how filthy her shirt was, and let it drop. She took a long swallow from the bottle and set it back on the table, giving Viola a nod of thanks. Ebba and Ottilie were sitting at the far corner of the table, heads close together as they talked in low voices, their hands clasped together in a knot. Ruth was going through the stack of ration packets, occasionally showing one to Clementine, who would only shake her head no.

Viola went back to the bar to stroke the cat's head, although Tubbins had gone to sleep long ago.

"Is he going to be okay?" Scout asked when Warrior came back to the bar.

"Maybe," Warrior said, sounding tired. "Sleeping is normal. It takes a lot of energy to heal."

Scout had a ton more questions, more about the galactic center than about the cat, and really wanted to know about the fugitive from justice that Warrior was hunting. Was it one of the rebels? But Shadow was pawing at her knee, a gesture she well knew the meaning of.

"I should take the dogs up the tunnel a bit," she said.

At the word "dogs," Girl began to thump her tail again, but hesitantly, as if she wasn't sure if she was still in trouble or not.

"Not the tunnel," Viola said, lurching away from the bar. She crossed one of the shelves and pulled out a tote, tossing the lid aside so she could dig through the contents. "Here," she said, thrusting what looked like a folded blanket at Scout. Scout crossed the room to take it. It wasn't a blanket; the surface felt papery, but it was thick and felt like it was full of beads. "Take them two rooms down that way," Viola said, pointing to one of the doorways. "That's where the cat goes. Have them go on this. I trust if it's not liquid, you'll dispose of it yourself. There's a toilet in the corner."

"Yes, of course. Thank you," Scout said. Viola said nothing, just stomped back to her cat. Scout gave a little whistle, and the dogs followed her.

As soon as she stepped through the doorway, the room beyond detected her presence and the light came on. This room was rectangular, longer than wide, and used for storage—and, if anything, dustier than the octagonal room. She passed through the far doorway and another light came on. Now she was in a locker room with a few showers and toilet stalls in the far corner. Everything was built for function and durability only: not a single splash of color, just metal lockers, concrete walls, too-bright lights, and tile floors that had probably once been white but were fading to a gray that matched the concrete. Even the benches of molded plastic were gray; no faux-wood here.

She could smell the cat box from the doorway. So could the dogs. Shadow stopped in his tracks when she told him to leave it, but she had to grab Girl by the collar and pull her away. She spread the pad on the floor.

"Shadow, come here," she said, pointing to the pad. He was hesitant, touching just a toe and then a paw before pulling away to sit down on the cold stone floor and look up at her questioningly. She patted the pad again and called him one more time. She could see in his eyes he knew what she meant, and if a dog could sigh, she was sure he would be doing that now. At last, he stood up and came over to her and lifted his leg.

Girl was halfway back to the cat box and Scout had to catch her collar again and pull her over to the pad. She didn't seem to mind the feel of it under her feet, and once she saw what Shadow was doing, she followed suit.

When Scout and the dogs got back to the main room, everyone was in the process of putting together a meal on the long table. Viola's bottle had been put away, and Ebba and Ottilie were setting out aluminum plates, cups, and flatware. The ration packets were nowhere to be seen. The room directly across from Scout was now lit up and she could see she had been right about what she heard. Three refrigerators stood in a row, one with a glass front through which she could see an array of beverages, including her favorite brand of jolo. As she drew closer, she could see there was also a massive stove and a row of ovens. Ruth was in that corner, watching something cook inside a microwave.

Warrior and Viola were still at the bar with the cat, and Girl ran over to them, whimpering because the cat was out of reach. Viola made a growling sound low in her throat and Girl backed away.

The microwave beeped and Ruth took out a covered tureen and brushed past Scout as she carried it to the table. Scout edged closer to the refrigerators. It looked like Viola was sharing her food. What about the jolo?

Then, as she passed a doorway on her left, something caught the corner of her eye. She took half a step back, as if afraid of being caught, although she hadn't been doing anything yet. She drew up to the edge of the doorway, peeking around the corner to see Liv in her hover chair, tightly grasping Clementine's forearm to pull her closer as she spoke to her in a voice so low Scout couldn't even hear a murmur of it.

What could Liv have to say to Clementine? The girl never spoke.

But then Scout saw the girl nod her head. That was more response than Scout had seen her giving even Ruth.

Scout jumped at a hand on her shoulder and turned to see Ruth smiling at her. "Hungry?"

"I guess so," Scout said.

"It's just freeze-dried soup, but it smells pretty good," Ruth said, still smiling. "Have you seen Clementine?"

"Yeah," Scout said. "She's in there. With Liv."

Ruth's eyebrows came together in mild confusion, but her smile didn't falter. "Well, you should go get it while it's hot." Then she went through the doorway into the room where Clementine was now standing quite apart from Liv. Ruth went to her, putting a hand on each of her shoulders and steering her back to the main room. Liv followed, glancing up at Scout still hovering near the doorway.

"Do I know you from somewhere?" Liv asked her.

"No, I would remember you," Scout said.

"Yes, I suppose you would," Liv said. "Still..."

She stared at Scout's face as if cataloguing every detail, a slight frown to the corners of her mouth. Then she gave herself a shake and continued on to the table.

Scout had definitely never met her. Even without the chair, she had never seen eyes so piercing. They were rapacious. Like she hunted from on high. But perhaps Scout was not the one Liv thought she remembered.

Everyone had always told Scout that she looked exactly like her mother. Had Liv known *her*?

11

THE OTHERS HAD GATHERED around the table, Viola filling bowls of soup from the now-uncovered tureen as Ruth passed around a basket filled with a variety of bread rolls. Ottilie seized her spoon as if it were some sort of shoveling tool and began eating her soup with gusto. Ebba beside her was more delicate, carefully blowing off each spoonful before bringing it to her lips. Clementine was tearing a roll into small pieces and dropping them into her soup. For a moment, it looked like a family reunited after many years, a little awkward with each other but still feeling the bonds of kin. Only Warrior, off to the side, still nursing the sick cat, didn't quite fit the picture.

Scout wasn't sure she fit either. The only space left at the table was next to where Liv had parked her hover chair. Scout sat down and took the bowl Viola handed her.

"Thank you," she said. "Really. I know we're an intrusion."

Viola made a grunt that could have meant anything. "I apologize for the rude welcome. I don't get many visitors. I don't like visitors. Still, it's not the way my parents raised me. I have enough to share. Please eat all you like."

"What is this place?" Scout asked, as she reached for the basket of rolls. "You look like a supply depot, but you're so hidden away."

"My customers know how to find me," Viola said. "My grandparents started this business from the early days. It was still booming in my parents' day. Not so much now."

"Speaking of parents," Liv said from Scout's other side, "where are yours?"

"Dead since the war," Scout said, she hoped forcefully enough that Liv would drop the matter.

"Soldiers?" Liv asked.

"Civilians," Scout said. "They were in Sunshine Valley."

Viola and Liv both sucked in a long breath. "I'm so sorry," Liv said, reaching out to grasp Scout's hand.

"That must've been hard for you," Viola said. "What were you, twelve?"

"Ten," Scout said. "I've done okay."

"Sunshine Valley," Liv said as she chewed a bit of bread. "A lot of communications officers were stationed there."

"My parents worked in communications, before I was born," Scout said. "They left the military to start a bakery."

"And you were away the day the rock fell," Liv guessed.

"Rock fell," Ruth said bitterly. "Nice. Like it just happened to happen."

"We all know how it happened," Viola said.

"And we all know who made it happen," Ruth said.

"You know, I'm getting a little tired of all this," Ottilie said. "Your daddy's been on about it for years now, and what good does it do?"

"What good does it do?" Ruth repeated, and Scout could sense a lengthy lecture coming on. She wasn't entirely annoyed when Liv clutched her hand to get her attention. Liv gestured with her hand for Scout to lean in closer.

"I'm just wondering—is it possible I knew your parents?" Liv asked.

"I don't know. Were you familiar with the bakers of Sunshine Valley?" Scout asked.

"No, I think I knew them from before then. From my work in communications."

"Not in Sunshine Valley."

"Yes, actually. I had been transferred to the capital just two weeks before that day," Liv said. "But I think I remember your parents. Your father, his name was… Antonio? He had dark, thick, curly hair and a great big smile. Your mother, I don't remember as well. She was so quiet. But she had your eyes." Liv reached up and pushed back Scout's hat. She lifted the sweat-dampened curls off of Scout's brow. "And your hair. It's hard to tell in this light, but I bet it shines like honey in the sun."

"I don't know, it's hard for me to see it," Scout said. But it felt like a fist was squeezing her heart. She truly didn't look at her own hair much, but her mother's she remembered very well. It had indeed shone like honey in the sun.

"They were working with the rebels, weren't they?" Liv said, leaning closer still to whisper directly in Scout's ear. She pulled back and gave Scout a knowing smile. Scout felt like her ears were ringing, like the whole rest of the room had faded away. Could it be true?

"They were bakers," Scout said, but not as certainly as she would have liked.

Liv looked her over very carefully, as if the truth of the past were written on her face. She smiled again and gave Scout's hand a pat. "As you like, dear."

"If they had been spies, they would've left the city. Right?" she asked.

"Perhaps you're right," Liv said, turning her attention back to her food. "It was a long time ago. I'm probably misremembering. And it was all just rumors, anyway."

Scout looked down at her food, no longer hungry. Why was Liv bringing it up if it all had just been rumors?

But maybe it hadn't been. She remembered again that momentary look on her father's face. Had he known?

The argument at the other end of the table had also ground to a halt, apparently with many bad feelings all around. The muscles in Ottilie's arms were tense, her grip on her spoon so tight her knuckles were white. Ebba was looking at her with fond concern. Ruth looked like she might burst into tears, but had no one to comfort her. Clementine was ignoring everything around her, poking with her spoon into a bowl that was more bread than soup. Viola also seemed unconcerned with the others around her, ladling more soup into a bowl and helping herself to another crusty roll.

Scout got up from the table, nearly tripping over Shadow, who had been lurking near her feet. She gave him the uneaten half of her roll, then went over to the bar where Warrior was sitting alone next to the cat. The cat was quite asleep, and Girl had also conked out, limbs sprawled everywhere behind the bar. Warrior had that strange tablet in her hands again, thumbs moving over invisible keys with dizzying speed.

"How's Tubbins doing?" Scout asked.

"Well enough," Warrior said, not looking up from her tablet.

"I guess you weren't hungry," Scout said.

"I don't eat much," Warrior said. This time, she glanced up at Scout briefly. "Did you eat?"

"Some. I wasn't really hungry," Scout said.

"Filled up on biscuits back in the rover, eh?" Warrior said.

"Something like that."

Warrior glanced up at her again. There wasn't much to that movement. It was impossible to track her eyes behind those lenses, but Scout could see her chin move up just a bit and knew when Warrior was looking at her and, as it moved back down, when she wasn't. "Something bothering you, kid?"

"Liv said my parents were spies."

"Ah," Warrior said. "That must be startling to hear from a stranger."

Scout couldn't tell whether Warrior was teasing her or not. She decided to assume not. "It might make sense, though."

"You'll have to tell me how that makes sense," Warrior said, her thumbs over the invisible keys never slowing.

"There're just so many coincidences," Scout said.

"You mean the eight of us all finding each other out here where people generally aren't?"

"Partly," Scout said. "Not just that, though. You know there was a war here."

"I've gathered as much."

"It ended six years ago. The Space Farers caught three asteroids and threw them down from orbit. One of them landed on my hometown."

Warrior finally set the tablet down, resting her hands on her knees as she gave Scout her full attention.

"I wasn't there that day. Obviously," Scout added. "My father sent me away. He sent me on a delivery, by myself, to the next town. He had never done that before."

Warrior seemed to think about this for a minute. "So you think that means he was a spy?"

"Why else would he send me away?"

"You were what, ten?" Scout nodded. "Ten. Old enough for a little responsibility. Any siblings?"

"I had a baby brother. Not yet one."

"And you had done deliveries before?"

"Only in town. He bought me a bike—not the one I have now, a different one. It had a basket in front and another in back, and I delivered bread and other things all over town. But only in town."

Warrior looked down at Shadow, now at Scout's heel, having finished the bread. "And you had your dog with you."

"He always came with me. Our town was safe, but sometimes my father worried."

"Well, do you want my opinion, kid?" Warrior asked, sitting back on the barstool.

"Yeah," Scout said.

"It sounds to me like your father just thought you'd shown yourself capable of more responsibility. You being gone that day of all days? That was just bad timing. Like you said, coincidence."

"But if he had been a spy—"

"If I were you, kid, I'd want some proof before I believed such a thing," Warrior said, reaching for her tablet.

"It's not so crazy," Scout said. Warrior just shrugged. "And it *is* weird, all eight of us being out here. There is nothing here to make people come out this way. Just the rebels, really."

"I can't speak for Liv, and maybe not for Ruth or Clementine either, but the rest of us are only out here because we followed the beacon."

"I don't know. I just feel like maybe I was meant to be out here," Scout said, thrusting her hands deep in the pockets of her cargo shorts and avoiding the glare from those reflective lenses.

"How's that?"

"There must've been a reason I wasn't home that day. And if there was a reason for that, then there must be a reason I'm here, now."

"Kid, I haven't been all over the galaxy, but I've seen more than my fair share. One thing I can tell you: reasons like the ones you're looking for are rare things. Mostly, you just deal with what's in front of you and hope for the best."

"What's in front of me now?" Scout asked.

"Well, the solar flare for one," Warrior said. "If I were you, I'd be a little curious why someone wants you to think your parents were spies. That's a weird thing to tell someone you just met."

"Can you tell me why you're chasing this fugitive?" Scout asked. "Does it really have nothing to do with the rebels?" Or with her or her parents, she wanted to add, but didn't.

"I really can't tell you. But I *can* tell you it's got nothing to do with any of you, I promise."

"I suppose it's a much bigger matter than the war on my little world," Scout said bitterly.

"Bigger? I don't know. It's just a different thing. I don't go in much for comparisons," Warrior said.

Warrior's blank slab of a tablet made a sudden trilling noise. She picked it up and looked at it intently. There was another noise coming from somewhere else in the room, a repeated beeping. Viola got up from the table and headed to the doorway directly across from the tunnel they'd entered from. The light came on as she stepped inside and Scout could see walls lined with equipment, panels of buttons, and screens filled with information displayed so small she could read it from where she was.

"What is it?" Ottilie asked. "Another storm warning?"

"No," Viola said over her shoulder as she scanned the screen. "This is from the planetary news service."

"They've declared a state of emergency?" Liv asked.

Scout was wondering the same thing. A piece of news that set off the alarms—what could it be short of war?

"No," Viola said as she strolled back into the room. Her eyes were on Ruth, and one by one, they all looked at Ruth as well.

Ruth had her fingertips pressed to her temples, resting her elbows on the table. She didn't look good. She hadn't looked good when they picked her up, but she was much worse now.

"So, what was the news?" Ottilie asked.

"Someone has been declared a traitor and a spy. She's wanted by the authorities. They are asking for any information on her whereabouts. She's been declared so dangerous they're willing to travel even through the solar flare to retrieve her." Viola leaned in behind Ruth to whisper loudly, "Seems she didn't just betray her government; she's betrayed her own family."

12

A HUSH FELL over the room. Warrior moved to stand at the head of the table, opposite Liv. Scout followed, Shadow close at her side. Ebba clasped Ottilie's hand and Ottilie squeezed back. Clementine's eyes moved around the table from one of them to the next, but her face was inscrutable. Was she looking for allies for herself and Ruth, or was she looking to change loyalties, to find a new patron to protect her? When her gaze fell on Scout, she just stared back, trying to put all her disdain into her eyes. Clementine smirked ever so slightly, then looked briefly at Liv at the end of the table.

Liv was leaning forward, elbows resting on the arms of her chair and fingers steepled under her chin, waiting with rapt attention for Ruth to speak.

Viola remained standing just behind Ruth, towering over her with her arms crossed. Ruth seemed to have collapsed in on herself, her entire body shaking as if she had caught a chill.

"Please," she said, her teeth all but chattering. "Please, you don't understand."

"What don't we understand?" Ottilie asked.

"You were right," Ruth said, dropping her hands to look directly at Ottilie. "You're right that war is coming. You're right that my father wants to see it happen. All of this 'Planet Dwellers first' talk? He knows that's going to lead to war."

"I've heard that same talk from you," Ottilie said.

"I had to play along," Ruth said earnestly. "Don't you remember what happened to my brother?"

"The official word was that he was resting," Ottilie said. It was clear from how she stressed that last word what she thought of that explanation.

"He's under house arrest, at our family ranch way out west," Ruth said, her voice cracking. "I haven't seen him in years. For all I know, he's already dead."

"Why are they looking for you now?" Scout asked.

"I… took some things. Information. Intelligence."

"So you are a spy," Viola said, almost smugly.

"Yes, maybe, but not for the Space Farers."

"You were going to give it to the rebels," Scout guessed.

"I was going to talk to them," Ruth said. "I've been in communication with them for some time now, but I'm not sure they can be trusted. I have important information, and I want to stop the war, but I'm not sure who to turn to. The Space Farers I've spoken with say all the right things, but there's just something in their eyes. I'm afraid they want war as much as my father does. The rebels don't want war, but I'm not sure what they do want. I just came here to talk to them." Then she gave a humorless laugh. "Bad timing."

"Maybe we should see what you have," Ottilie said.

"No," Ruth said, shaking her head repeatedly.

"How can we judge whether or not to trust you if we don't see what you have?" Ottilie persisted.

"Please," Ruth pleaded.

"Perhaps we should look at this from another angle," Warrior said.

"What do you mean?" Viola asked.

"Reporting Ruth would mean bringing government officials here, in the middle of the storm. Is that something everyone here is cool with?" Her reflective lenses bore down on them all.

"She might have a point," Ottilie said reluctantly.

"Damn right she's got a point," Viola said. "I don't need more people in here."

"I promise you, nothing I have is going to draw danger down on any of you," Ruth said.

"Well, I don't know about that," Viola said. "They're still going to be looking for you once the flare passes. I imagine they'll follow you here."

"I'll be out the door the minute it's safe to go outside," Ruth promised. "I just need a little head start."

"If you want to report her, tip them off and get your reward—can you wait until the flare passes? Give the rest of us a head start too," Ottilie said.

"Who said anything about a reward?" Viola asked.

"There's always a reward," Ottilie said. Viola just chuckled.

"So we're agreed?" Warrior said.

Ottilie and Ebba readily nodded. Viola waved a hand dismissively. Clementine was as silent as ever, but then she was hardly likely to raise an alarm, was she? Scout nodded when Warrior turned those lenses on her. Only Liv seemed still pensive, chin resting on her fingertips.

"Liv?" Warrior asked.

"Hmm? Oh, yes. No need for authorities if you're all so jumpy about it," Liv said, but she still seemed lost in her thoughts. Scout wondered if she was just deflecting, pretending to defer to the others as if it didn't matter to her. How had she gotten out here, all alone in a hover chair, and why?

"Thank you," Ruth said. "You'll all understand later what this means. I truly believe by letting me go you're saving lives, not just on the planet, but also up in orbit."

As if needing to prove herself useful, she pushed away from the table and began gathering dishes to carry back to the kitchen. Ebba got up to help her, and Scout reached for the bread basket.

"Do we bed down here?" Ottilie asked, looking around the room. There was certainly room enough for each of them to spread out a bedroll or curl up in a blanket.

"Can do," Viola said, "but you'd be more comfortable in the barracks, I think."

"That does sound more comfortable," Ottilie agreed.

Scout brought the bread basket into the kitchen and set it on one of the counters. Ruth was loading dishes into a washer, and Ebba was scraping the last of the soup into a storage container. Scout looked longingly at the refrigerator, but it was the completely wrong time of day for jolo. If she had one now, she'd be up all night. And she was feeling worn out. She had biked only a fraction of the distance she did in a normal day, but pedaling at full speed with Warrior's weight as well as her own had taken its toll. She didn't want jolo alertness now; she wanted deep, restful sleep.

The others were trickling out of the kitchen, following a lighted path past the communications room to a long, narrow room lined with bunks.

"What is this place, really?" Scout asked, pausing in the middle room to look over all the screens. There were cameras posted at several entrances, and a blank screen over the door Ottilie had blown open with the mining charge that Scout guessed was from a camera. Another screen was charting the coronal mass ejection with even greater detail than Warrior's little device. Scout leaned in to read some of the text. "You're getting feeds from space?"

"Yeah," Viola said. "My equipment predates the war, and no one bothered to lock me out of anything. I'm not sure if they even know I'm down here. This was a way station for the early explorers. The entrance to the hangar for rover storage is buried now, but everything still works."

"We followed your beacon. It's still signaling," Scout said.

"My grandparents stayed on here after the city domes were completed. This wasn't really needed as a way station for explorers anymore, but it became a supply post for those sorts who aren't really town-living folks. My parents kept it up, and now me. Not too many customers these days, but enough to get by."

"Where's Ebba?" Ottilie asked, poking her head into the communications room from the barracks.

"Still in the kitchen, maybe?" Scout said, looking back into the main room. Warrior was still there, running her hands over the cat. Girl was sitting up, ears all cockeyed as she blinked sleepily at the activity around her.

"Can Tubbins be moved?" Viola asked, brushing past Scout to get to the bar.

"I should think so," Warrior said. "He's going to sleep pretty deeply until the nanite is done working, and he'll be groggy for a bit after that. But no reason you can't keep him near you." Warrior scooped up the sleeping cat and poured him into Viola's waiting arms.

"I'm so sorry for this," Scout said, but Viola just nodded, clutching her cat close to her chest and passing through the communications room and barracks to her private space beyond. "Come on, Girl," she said, and Girl got clumsily to her feet.

Ebba and Ottilie were packed together in one narrow bunk near the door. Ruth was getting Clementine settled on the opposite side of the room one bed further on. Liv had moved herself from her chair to the bottom bunk two beds down from Ebba and Ottilie and was using a handheld device to direct her chair to park itself at the open space near the closed door to Viola's room.

Scout frowned at the zigzag pattern of the taken beds. Clearly no one wanted to be right next to anyone else, but there were no more open beds a bunk apart from the others. She was going to be annoying somebody, whatever her choice.

"You should take a top bunk," Warrior said from behind where she was hesitating in the doorway.

"With the dogs?"

"Precisely. We need to be sure they don't go wandering about looking for more trouble. If they try to get down from up there, they'll wake you doing it."

Scout could see this was true. Shadow could make such a jump, but Girl would likely break something. She picked up Shadow first and put him up on the bunk near the door, across from Ebba and Ottilie, but once she was up in it, they'd be out of sight from each other. Warrior helped her hoist the squirming Girl up, then Scout pulled herself up after.

"Where are you going to be?" she asked Warrior.

"I don't sleep much," Warrior said. "I'll probably pass the time in the communications room, watching information flow."

"And standing guard?" Scout guessed.

"That too."

They were both distracted by a soft whining sound that turned out to be coming from Clementine; it seemed she didn't want Ruth to leave her even to move to the bed directly across the corridor. Ruth gave in with a sigh, lying down at the very edge of the bed. She didn't look comfortable, and Scout doubted she'd get much sleep while balancing like that. Ottilie and Ebba were tucked in together like spoons and seemed to be already fast asleep. But Scout couldn't fault Ruth for not wanting to cuddle up to that strange little girl.

"Good night," Warrior said, patting Scout's knee before turning to head back into the communications room. Scout took off her boots and set them on a shelf that ran alongside the bunk, built into the wall of the room. She put her hat next to it, then slipped off her father's shirt and wadded it up before stuffing it on the shelf too. Shadow was already pawing at the blanket and sheet, wanting to get under the covers. Girl was not so picky. She waited for Scout to get herself and Shadow situated in the bedding, then flopped down at the foot of the bunk, her head on Scout's ankle. She seemed to be looking into the communications room, the light from the screens reflecting off her eyes.

A moment later, now that everyone had gone still, the barracks light shut off with a soft click and the greenish glow from those screens was the only light in the room. Scout tucked an arm under her head.

She had slept in caves before, but never so far underground. She tried to guess how deep they were, remembering the sloping corridor that had taken them down this way, then the spiral staircase. But it was hard to judge; the land here was still rolling hills, and the entrance they had found had been at the top of one of those hills. If they weren't under a hill now, they might not be all that deep.

Surely there'd be more time for exploring in the morning, especially now that Viola was bending and even becoming welcoming. Perhaps there'd even be jolo.

Scout slipped into a restful sleep, her hand on Shadow's warm belly, feeling the soft rise and fall as he breathed.

Then there was a thump, and the air was full of screams.

13

WARRIOR CHARGED into the room and the lights snapped back on. Scout kept Shadow tucked close to her and leaned out into the room to see Ruth lying facedown on the floor. Well, that had been inevitable, precariously perched as she had been.

Only Ruth wasn't moving. And someone was still screaming, one continuous blast of sound without seeming to need to draw breath.

"Stop it," Warrior said calmly as she knelt by Ruth's side. "Calm yourself."

Girl was growling, her hackles rising into a terrifying ridge of black fur. Ebba got out of her bunk and crossed over to sit on the edge of Clementine's bunk, pulling the girl into a tight hug. At last, the screaming stopped as suddenly as it had begun.

"She's dead," Scout said. Warrior nodded.

"How?" Liv demanded.

The door to Viola's room snapped open and Viola stood there in a flannel nightgown and a fierce scowl that only deepened when she saw Warrior kneeling over Ruth's still form.

"What happened?" she demanded.

"I don't know," Warrior said to both of them. "But she's dead. Cold already, even."

"Natural causes?" Ebba asked softly. "She really didn't look well."

"No, she didn't," Warrior agreed. "I can test for a few things. I'll bring her out to the table so I can get a better look."

"Not the table. We eat on that!" Viola said. "She'll fit on the bar, like the cat."

Warrior gathered Ruth up into her arms, turning her over in the process. Her hair spilled around with the movement, covering her face like a veil but leaving slashes of exposed skin that looked bluish under the barracks light.

Scout's heart clenched coldly. As much as her life was defined by those she loved being dead, she had never been near a dead body before.

Scout kicked back the blankets and reached for her boots. The others were getting up as well, Liv summoning her hover chair as Ottilie went to stand by Ebba's shoulder.

"We should give her something," Ottilie said, pointing at Clementine with her chin.

"Sleeping pill?" Viola asked.

"I was thinking hot chocolate," Ottilie said.

"With a splash of brandy," Viola said, not quite under her breath. "I can go the rest of my life without hearing that scream again. Thank you."

"She's not likely to do that again," Ebba said, pulling the blanket off the bed to wrap around the girl like a shawl, then keeping an arm around her shoulders to guide her back to the kitchen.

Clementine looked up at Scout as she passed the bunk, almost smirking. Strange reaction to having one's guardian die suddenly while lying next to you on the same bed. Girl's ongoing growl deepened and Scout put a hand on her head to calm her. Viola was glaring up at the two of them, and Scout leaned over to whisper softly to Girl until she quieted. Only then did Viola follow the others back out to the main room.

Scout put on her shirt and hat and jumped down to the floor to lift the dogs down one by one. They stayed close at her heels through the communications room to the main room beyond. Scout fought back another wave of cold revulsion and made herself cross the room to stand by Warrior's elbow and watch as she studied the screen of a device shaped like a table standing on needles, which she had stabbed into Ruth's now-exposed belly.

"That will tell you what killed her?" Scout asked.

"Maybe, if it was something obvious," Warrior said. "In my line of work, most causes of death are one of the obvious ones, but you never know when you'll run into something way too unique."

"Like what?" Scout asked, but Warrior didn't seem to hear her.

"I was afraid of that," she said.

"Afraid of what?" Ottilie asked, trying to examine the screen for herself, but nothing was labeled. It was just an array of colored lines and dots.

"Poison," Warrior said.

"But there's not a mark on her," Ottilie said, picking up Ruth's arms to examine the pale skin. "It could be just a pinprick, but still."

"Scout, give me your arm," Warrior said. Scout readily complied. Warrior had something smaller in her hand that pricked a needle into Scout's arm, but it was done and she had turned away before Scout could even hiss in a breath from the pain. "Yes, I was afraid that's what it was."

"I'm poisoned too?" Scout asked.

"We all are," Ottilie said, not a guess.

Warrior nodded, still studying her screen.

"There was soup left over in the kitchen," Scout said, rubbing at the spot on her arm where the machine had pricked her. There was no blood, only a tiny red dot on her skin like a cherry-colored freckle.

"I can check that. But don't worry, you didn't get a fatal dose," Warrior said.

"What if I ate more than her?" Ottilie asked.

"I can test you," Warrior said.

"I have antidotes in my medical stores," Viola said. "Give me the name of the poison and we can all take a dose, just to be sure."

"How did she die if we all got a nonfatal dose?" Scout asked as Warrior pricked Ottilie's arm and watched the results on the screen.

"Perhaps an underlying condition," Warrior said.

"She did look ill," Ottilie said. "I've seen her on video feeds before, and she doesn't usually look so malnourished."

"But what does this mean? Who poisoned all of us?" Scout asked. "Is someone in here with us? Someone who followed her out here, trying to kill her? Someone from the rebel group she was trying to meet up with?"

"There's no one here but you," Viola said.

"But how can you be sure?" Ottilie asked.

"I saw you all come in, or I did until you took out the camera."

"Cameras can be worked around," Warrior said. "Bypassed or slipped past. It happens all the time. Which doesn't make it the most likely scenario," she added. She showed the screen to Viola, who nodded and marched off toward the locker room and showers. The medical supplies were down that arm of the complex, Scout guessed.

"What about what Ruth knew?" Scout asked. "She must have had proof. A data file or something."

"You can look for it if you like," Warrior said. "I'm not sure if it really matters. Facts so rarely do in things like this."

Viola came back with a loaded vaccination gun and pressed it to her own biceps while Scout and Warrior watched, flinching as she fired a dose into her own flesh. Then she reached for Scout's arm.

"I'll be fine without it," Warrior said.

"I bet you will," Viola said. "Didn't your nanites give you a warning you'd ingested poison?"

"She didn't eat anything," Scout said, realizing as she said it that it was true.

"That's suspicious," Viola said, narrowing her eyes.

"Not really," Warrior said blandly. "I require little sustenance, and when I do, I have my own supply of high-nutrient liquid. Can't remember the last time I chewed anything."

"Ew. Also, kinda sad," Scout said. Warrior just shrugged.

Ottilie summoned Ebba and Clementine out of the kitchen and Viola gave them each a shot, lastly Liv, who had remained in the communications room studying the screens.

"I watched the playback on all the camera feeds since the beginning of the storm," Liv said. "No one is in here but us. Which means one of us is a poisoner."

"I told you so," Viola said.

"It was your food, and you made it pretty clear you didn't want us here," Liv said.

"I ate the same as the rest of you. She didn't," Viola said, pointing to Warrior.

"I have no motive," Warrior said.

"Who does?" Scout asked.

"Who has motive? Now, with war about to break out? The dead woman being someone carrying information to take down her own government? I think that should be pretty obvious," Liv said, glaring at Ebba.

"Not on your life," Ottilie said, moving to stand between Ebba and her accuser. "The war is over for us, and it always will be. We're done."

"We can point fingers at each other all night, but it's not going to solve anything," Warrior said. "You can summon your government officials when the storm breaks and they can run an investigation. They'll have the equipment and the capability to track the history of the poison, find the buyer or at least the seller. They can get to the bottom of this."

"This storm is supposed to last for four days," Viola pointed out.

"I guess we won't be sleeping much, now that we know we're all trapped here with a murderer," Ottilie said.

"I'll make some coffee," Ebba said.

"I'll do it," Viola said. "No one else goes in my kitchen. I'm program-ming the doors with alarms and countermeasures. No one leaves this room but me."

"Quite reasonable," Warrior said. "For the rest of you, I can test the coffee before you drink it if you're worried Viola is the poisoner."

"That means trusting you too," Liv said. "I'm not sure I do."

"All you're trusting is that Viola and I aren't in league together. Do the math. Or don't have coffee, I don't care."

"What about the body?" Ottilie asked. They all looked at Ruth still laid out on the bar, that strange device perched on her bare stomach.

"Wrap her in a sheet," Viola said, waving a hand dismissively.

Warrior picked Ruth back up and carried her back to the barracks to lay her on one of the bunks. She fussed over her briefly, then came back to the common room, tucking her device away in its place on her belt.

Viola went into the communications room to reprogram the doors. Scout caught her on the way out of that room to the kitchen. "What about the dogs? Are these countermeasures dangerous?"

"Keep them close with you," Viola said shortly, then headed into the kitchen. An invisible barrier across the doorway lit up green as she passed through it and returned to invisibility.

Scout went back to the shelf where Viola had gotten the thick pad for the dogs to do their business on and took another one down to spread close to one wall near the bar. It was the closest thing to a mattress she was likely to find. The dogs scrambled to curl up close to her as she flopped down, still exhausted from the long day.

"Get some sleep, kid," Warrior said, pulling one of the barstools over to sit near the pad. "I'll keep watch. You trust me, right?"

"I do," Scout admitted. Girl was already conked out, head on Scout's ankles, but Shadow was fussing over the lack of blanket. He would just have to sleep out in the open for one night, fussy as he was. She stroked around his ears, keeping her head down but certain that even at a whisper Warrior would hear her. "There was someone else, someone no one pointed a finger at."

"They were all thinking it," Warrior said, barely loud enough for Scout to hear.

"Clementine," she said anyway. "She is creepy, and Girl doesn't like her. Not a bit. Shadow barks at anything and everything, but not Girl. She's more selective."

"I've noticed that. And yet you keep telling me she's not all that bright," Warrior said.

"I don't know. I guess I trust her gut instinct," Scout said.

Warrior didn't say anything for a long time, just watched as the others got settled on the floor. Clementine was still clinging to Ebba as her new protector, despite Ottilie's palpable annoyance. The back of Liv's hover chair hummed as it moved to a nearly horizontal position, and from somewhere inside the thing she produced a light lap blanket that she drew around her shoulders. Then a canopy slipped over the top, enclosing her as if in an egg. Scout guessed she'd feel pretty safe inside such a thing as well.

Viola emerged from the kitchen with a self-heating samovar of coffee, which she plunked down on the table before retreating back to her own room, to her bed and her comatose cat, the doorways flashing green as she passed through them.

Ottilie got up from the floor, fished a mug out of her bag, and filled it from the samovar, then brought it to Warrior perched on the barstool. She held it out without comment and Warrior plucked a gadget from her belt and aimed it at the mug's contents, then gave a sharp nod. Ottilie nodded back in thanks, then returned to her position on the floor, now with a steaming mug in her hands.

Scout's eyes were getting heavy, and Shadow's deep, even breathing and the warmth of his form tucked against her belly were wooing her to sleep.

"I don't have an official capacity on this planet," Warrior said, her voice pitched even lower than before. Scout suspected some sort of ventriloquist's trick, throwing her voice to where only Scout could hear it.

"You're saying this isn't your problem?" Scout asked in a whisper.

"No more than it's yours. If the girl has been poisoning her guardian, is that our concern?"

"She poisoned all of us, though."

"To get to Ruth. I don't think she's likely to do it again. In the meantime, we keep an eye on her, keep her away from the food and water, wait out the storm. The planetary authorities can have her then."

"You're saying don't confront her?" Scout asked.

"I don't see a reason to. Firstly, we have no real proof. But secondly, we know she's a threat; she probably knows we know. Enough said."

Scout was too tired to argue. She could see that Warrior intended to stay awake, and Ottilie was sitting up with the posture of one also intending to stay up all night, eyes on Ebba even as Ebba attempted to soothe the emotionless Clementine.

"Keep your dogs close to you," Warrior said, her low voice

intruding even as Scout started to drift off to sleep. "I'll watch over you, but keep the dogs close."

"—m'kay," Scout mumbled, and she managed to wonder if her weariness were real or if she'd been drugged. What had been in that gun Viola had fired into all of them?

Then sleep took her.

14

SCOUT WOKE to a low murmur of voices. She felt like she had only just shut her eyes—not a full night's sleep by any means, but perhaps a decent, recharging sort of nap. The dogs were still out cold, both snuggled up close beside her. The air in the room felt colder than it had when she had laid down. She was used to that from nights when she slept outside. At least she wasn't damp with dew.

Warrior was still on the barstool, the featureless tablet again in her hands, although her thumbs were only occasionally poking at it. She tipped her head to glance back at Scout as she stirred.

Liv had converted her hover bed back to a chair and was at the table. Either she had also brought a mug with her inside her chair or she had found one around the room, but either way she was taking long swallows of coffee between long murmuring exchanges with Ottilie. Ottilie wasn't looking at her. She had moved from her spot on the floor to the bench at the table and was drinking coffee as well, but she never looked over at Liv even as she was obviously talking to her. Ebba and Clementine were still asleep against the far wall.

Scout carefully extricated herself from the dogs, encouraging them to huddle together for warmth. Then she stretched out the kinks as she walked to the table.

"Mugs are behind the bar," Warrior whispered to her as she passed.

"Thanks," Scout whispered back, going to retrieve one of a mismatched set and bringing it to the samovar. She expected the conversation to die away as she approached, but even though Liv clearly saw her coming, she continued speaking in a low, earnest voice.

"You don't know what she did," she was saying.

"I know more than you," Ottilie said, giving Scout the barest of glances. She hadn't responded to Liv up until this point. Like she didn't need to defend what Liv was attacking with unless there was someone else there to hear, and maybe to judge.

So Liv was accusing Ebba again of poisoning them all.

"I have as much reason as anyone to hate all Space Farers," Scout said softly as she filled her mug from the samovar. "But not Ebba."

"You've known her less than a day," Liv said.

"Longer than you," Scout said.

"I know more than you think I do, both of you," Liv said.

"Is this like how you knew my parents?" Scout asked skeptically.

"Yes," she said, then shook her head. "No, actually. What I know about your parents, it's just rumors and suspicions and a lot of things that would make so much sense if they were true. But this, I've seen proof with my own eyes."

"But you can't show this proof to me," Ottilie guessed.

"Obviously not. I don't have access to secure systems here. But I know I've seen her name in the Space Farer logs."

"She already told us she was in the military during the war," Scout said. Then, "Wait—how do you have access to Space Farer logs?"

"Some things have been… not exactly declassified, but open to lower security levels than before for us here planetside. My department is trying to assemble an official record of what happened, a history of sorts."

"Her name is going to be historical?" Scout asked. Ottilie looked like she had wanted to ask as well, and she shot Scout a look of gratitude for not making her ask Liv herself.

"Oh, yes. She was involved with many high-level ops."

"She was in communications," Ottilie said despite herself.

"Yes, she was," Liv said, smiling almost too widely with glee. "She communicated a great many things. She was an intermediary between intelligence gathering and tactical decision making, and between tactics and the front line."

"What does that mean?" Scout asked, glancing at Ottilie, who shrugged.

"Their chain of command is different from ours. I've never understood it, no matter how many times she's tried to explain," Ottilie admitted.

"Her job was like the spinal cord in a mammal, carrying signals to and from the brain, which is tactical administration, right?" Liv said, gesturing with her hands as she spoke. "But say you touch something hot and jerk your hand away. You pull your hand away before you even really feel the pain, right? That response happens so fast because it doesn't go all the way to your brain before you act. It goes just to the spinal cord, and the spinal cord sends the signal to pull away even before the brain processes the pain signals."

"And?" Ottilie said, growing impatient.

"The same thing was true with your friend Ebba. Sometimes, time was short, and she had to send out orders before hearing back from tactics." Liv glanced over at where Ebba and Clementine slept on, and Scout wondered just how much brandy had been dribbled in that hot chocolate and if they both had drunk it. Then Liv leaned forward. "There were several key attacks where the decision to move forward originated from her, not her higher-ups."

"It was wartime," Ottilie said dismissively.

"She gave the orders that took out Wayfarer Crossroads."

Ottilie hissed and turned red, almost as if Liv had slapped her. "You lie," she said, barely keeping her voice in check.

"What's Wayfarer Crossroads?" Scout asked. She had never heard of any such battle.

"One of the first places to be taken out by an asteroid dropped from space," Liv told her as Ottilie blinked back angry tears. "Some considered it a sort of proof of concept before the Space Farers started moving on to larger targets. Like the cities."

"Ebba did that?" Scout said doubtfully. "That doesn't sound like a snap decision. Not like you just described it with the spinal cord and everything."

"There was an underground factory in Wayfarer Crossroads. It was where the big guns were put together. They were just finishing up a sixth gun when Space Farer intelligence discovered their location. Perhaps they felt it was aimed at them. I don't know." She smirked again. "You could ask her, I suppose."

"Damn you," Ottilie growled.

Scout frowned. Ottilie had said so many times that the war was in their past, and yet this new information seemed to burn her in a personal way.

"Is that where your gun came from?" she asked.

"The gun, but also Ottilie herself," Liv said.

Ottilie cursed, long and prolific but still under her breath.

"How do you know this?" Scout demanded. "You whisper to me about my parents, you whisper to Ottilie about Ebba. All these accusations with no proof."

In the corner of her eye, she saw Ebba stirring at the sound of her name, and she realized she had neglected to keep her voice down.

"No proof? How do you think I know where you're from?" Liv said to Ottilie. Ebba was sitting up now, blinking sleepily at the three of them clustered at the table.

"My tattoo gives my squad," Ottilie said. "We were pretty much all from Wayfarer Crossroads. Not much of a stretch to guess I'd be from there, too."

"True enough," Liv allowed, looking over at Ebba and the slowly waking Clementine. "So, if you don't believe me, ask her."

"Ask me what?" Ebba asked anxiously. Ottilie's red face had deepened to scarlet, and Scout worried for the mug clutched so tightly in those scarred, muscled hands. But she did not speak. "Ottilie?" Ebba said.

"I told her about Wayfarer Crossroads. Apparently you never had," Liv said. "Just like a Space Farer to weasel in under cover of lies."

"You can't prove anything," Scout said hotly, but she fell silent at the look on Ebba's face. She had already been pale, but now she had gone paper-white. "Ebba?"

"What good does it do to rehash this now? The war is over," Ebba said to Liv. She rested her hands on Ottilie's shoulders, but Ottilie flinched away.

"Is what she's saying true?" she demanded.

"Ottilie, we agreed. The war is in the past," Ebba said desperately, reaching for her again.

Ottilie jumped to her feet to put space between them. "Yes, it's in the past, but it's not the furthest thing in the past." Ebba looked confused. "You knew when you dropped that rock that my entire family was there. You knew that was where I was from."

"Yes, of course I did," Ebba said, turning her hands palms up. "But you know—you've always known—it was a military target. It was a time of war. I know you understand this. The gun you fired—it could have struck one of the stations where my family lived as well. We knew that could happen. We always knew—" But her voice broke and she could say no more.

Ottilie was unmoved. "You knew my family was there. You knew I might be there as well." Ebba looked away, too quickly. "Didn't you? Or did you know I wasn't?"

"I knew you weren't," Ebba said, so low they could barely hear her. "I always, always, always knew where you were. I lived every day in fear of having to give an order that would put you in danger, and every night I thanked all the powers that be in the universe that that day hadn't been such a day."

"But my family. Collateral damage? Acceptable civilian casualties?"

Scout hugged herself tight. Those words—did the Space Farers use those words up in space to describe her family as well?

"Ottilie," Ebba pleaded, but Ottilie flinched at the sound of her own name. The sight of her recoiling made Ebba gasp. Then she turned and fled, the doorway flashing orange as she ran toward the showers.

"Viola didn't arm that one, I guess," Warrior said calmly as she watched Ebba disappear down the far end of the storage room.

"The bathrooms are down that way," Scout said. "Nice of her to leave us access without actually telling us."

"We're better off with her far away," Liv said.

Ottilie shot her a look of pure hate.

"If anyone wants my opinion, I think it's extremely unlikely that Ebba was out to harm anyone," Warrior said. "The war has scarred her; I guess now we know why. But she had put it in the past. You digging things up was a bit pointless. She wasn't the poisoner."

"We can't trust Space Farers," Liv said simply. "Never could, but now that the war is ramping up again, we definitely can't."

"I don't need you telling me who to trust," Scout said. "I know what my gut tells me, and I trust her a lot farther than I trust you."

She took a drink of coffee, looking over the rim at Clementine, still sleeping near the wall. Liv seemed like a muck-stirrer of the first order. What had she said to Clementine? Had it been so insidious, the girl would poison them all because of it? If only she'd gotten a little closer, a little sooner, and actually heard something.

Ottilie was taking long, slow breaths, moving step by step closer to Scout, away from Liv. Scout tried to give her an encouraging smile, but clearly what was troubling her soul was beyond such meager comforts.

"She probably shouldn't be wandering the place alone," Warrior said, getting up from the barstool and putting the tablet away. "Viola's safeguards, the possibility of another intruder lurking, just general mental well-being. We should find her."

"We?" Ottilie said weakly.

"You, me, Scout and the dogs. I'm thinking you should be there, but maybe not alone. In case she's upset. When we find her, maybe Scout and I can head back while the two of you take a moment. But we'll see where she's at when we find her."

"Thank you," Ottilie said.

"The doorways," Scout said with a vague wave of her hand.

"I'll scan each before we go through. Just keep your dogs close to you. A leash or two might not be a bad idea."

Scout looked around at the shelves, found one with stacks of coiled rope, and used the knife from her back pocket to cut off two lengths into makeshift leashes. Shadow had been leash-trained, although it had been a few years since he had worn one; the training would come back to him. Girl, on the other hand, was deeply confused and prone to lunging forward to half strangle herself.

"She'll get the hang of it," Scout said to Warrior, or perhaps mostly to herself.

Warrior just nodded and led the way through the first door, through the narrow storage room to the locker room and showers beyond. Ottilie followed, head down as if her thoughts were too heavy for her neck to support.

Scout looked back over her shoulder one last time. Clementine was still sitting on the floor, somewhere between asleep and awake, but Liv was already moving toward her in that silent hover chair, sliding into a position that blocked Clementine from Scout's view.

Scout just knew she was about to miss another mysterious conversation. She wished they had woken Viola to chaperone those two while they found Ebba.

Did Liv have information about Clementine's past as well?

15

THE DOORWAY between the second storage room and the locker room also flashed orange when they passed through it but didn't stop them in any way. Scout supposed that somewhere Viola was getting an alert every time they moved and knew exactly how many were in each room, and probably exactly who as well. She hadn't gotten even the smallest glimpse past the door to Viola's private rooms, but there must be a console or something in there with her and Tubbins.

The dogs saw the soiled pad still on the floor near the toilets and pulled toward it. She headed that way to let them do their business. Warrior walked along the far side of the room, looking between the rows of lockers. Ottilie hovered near the doorway uncertainly.

"Ebba?" Warrior called.

"I'm here," Ebba said. Scout had expected to find her in tears, but her voice gave no hint of it. "Come look at this."

Warrior waved for Ottilie to follow, then disappeared behind the last row of lockers. Scout decided to use the toilet herself while she waited for the dogs to finish. This necessitated dropping their leashes, but they didn't seem likely to dart off anywhere except possibly toward the litter box. When she was done, she disposed of the dogs' mess, washed her hands, and went to see what the other three were up to huddled in the back corner of the room.

Scout hadn't gone this far into the room the night before and was surprised to find the three of them clustered around a door standing ajar. It wasn't a full-sized door; even she would have to stoop to get through it.

"What's that?" she asked, holding the leashes more tightly as the dogs sniffed the air.

"Maintenance door," Warrior said, putting something back on her belt. "It doesn't seem to be locked or guarded in any way. But Viola must know it's here."

"It was open when I came back here," Ebba said. "Not all the way, just exactly as it is now. Only I thought I heard something moving around on the other side. I've been listening, but I haven't heard it again. Maybe I imagined it."

"Maybe," Warrior said, but she didn't sound like she believed it. She took the light off her belt and flashed it through the gap in the door. "There's a space inside the wall between this room and the next, and then another door. That one's open too. If someone is sneaking around the place, why are they being so careless?"

"Maybe it's not a person," Scout said. "Tubbins might not be the only cat. If Viola is worried about rodents, she might leave this open to let the cat hunt."

"Maybe," Warrior said, but again she didn't sound like she really believed it.

"Ebba," Ottilie started to say.

"I'm not ready to talk to you," Ebba said, an edge of hurt and anger to her voice that made Ottilie flinch away. "Should we check this out?" she asked Warrior.

"It's dark in there," Warrior said. "It's going to be hard to search if we can't find some lights. Hold on." She bent down to step through the door. The top of the doorframe caught the edge of her hat, pushing it back to dangle from where it was tied around her neck. She took another step, the door on the other side scraping loudly across the floor as she pushed it wider open.

"That might explain why it was left that way," Scout said. "Did you hear somebody leaving this room or just moving around on the other side?"

"Just movement," Ebba said. "Just for a moment. A kind of skitter, but I swear it was bigger than a cat."

They all bent and peered through the two doors to where Warrior's legs were visible, taking little steps as she turned in place, shining her light all around her.

"What is it?" Scout asked when she could no longer stand not knowing.

"A hangar," Warrior said. "Or it used to be. It looks like people kept abandoning things here until they choked up all the space. But it's huge. Huge and cluttered. It's going to be tough to search."

"Should we get the others?" Ottilie asked.

Warrior dropped to one knee to look back at them, her lenses more like inky pools in the darkness, barely reflecting. "No," she said at last. "It would be awkward for Liv to get in here, I'm not sure what use Clementine would be when she can't call out to the rest of us, and Viola… well, I'm not sure how we'd get her attention just now."

"Do you have flashlights in your bag from the rover?" Scout asked.

"No. There must be some here in one of those crates," Ottilie said, looking back the way they had come.

"I don't want to waste time digging. We can split into two groups. I can see well enough in the dark. The other group can take my light."

"I'll go with Warrior," Ebba said before Scout could speak. She took the light from Warrior's hand and gave it to Scout, not even looking at Ottilie.

"Okay then," Scout said.

"We'll head to the left. You two go right. Give a whistle if you find anything. And keep the dogs close to you. If it is another cat—"

"Got it," Scout said, double-wrapping the ends of the ropes around her hand and grasping them firmly. She handed the light to Ottilie, who followed Ebba through the doorway. Scout came last, herding the dogs through ahead of her.

At the other end, Warrior caught her arm to whisper in her ear. "Keep an eye out. It might just be a cat in here, but it might be more. Don't take this lightly."

"I won't," Scout promised. "Do you really think there's a person down here? Or more than one, like a hit squad sent to take out Ruth or something?"

"I wouldn't be that dramatic," Warrior said dryly. "I have been getting a sense of a… wrongness." She sounded almost embarrassed to have landed on that word.

"A wrongness?" Scout repeated. "Like a gut instinct?"

"More like something messing about at the very edge of my sensor's range and capabilities. It's unsettling. Just—err on the side of yelling over doing nothing. Got it, kid?"

"Got it," Scout said, then reached down to give Girl's side a quick pat. Shadow was sniffing the air intently. Scout wasn't sure if it was a good or bad thing that he seemed eager to lead them deeper into the dark to the right.

The space near the little door was open, but further along the wall were more shelves covered in crates and loose equipment. In the center of the space was larger equipment—farming and mining machinery, Scout guessed from what little she recognized. It was all covered in a thick blanket of dust, here and there disturbed by Tubbins's paw prints pursuing other, smaller paw prints. Sometimes the object would just be a thresher or something standing all on its own, its features softened under the blanket of dust, but other times there would be a thresher covered with rolls of tarp, crates both covered and uncovered, shapeless canvas sacks. Like someone had backed up a truck and tossed out everything they had been keeping in their shed and just left it here.

"If someone is in here, they picked the perfect place to hide," Scout said. "They could be anywhere."

"Can the dogs smell people? Like, track them?" Ottilie asked.

"I don't know. I've never used them for that before," Scout said.

The hangar seemed endlessly huge, although the further in they went, the more they had to take a winding path between heaps of junk. Ottilie played the light over everything before stepping around any of the junk piles. Occasionally they found more animal tracks on the floor, but mostly the only thing disturbing the dust was their own feet.

"I was about your age when I first met Ebba," Ottilie said to Scout in a low whisper. "We met at school, a boarding school in the city. The town I grew up in, Wayfarer Crossroads—it was pretty tiny. Of course, it's all gone now, nothing but a crater. Most of the people who lived there worked at the manufacturing plant, and there weren't many kids. I tested kind of bright, so I got sent to the city to study. But the kids there considered me a hick. I got teased. You know how kids are."

Scout didn't say anything. She hadn't been to a school since her family died, and her line of work didn't have her interacting with other kids much.

"But Ebba, being a Space Farer, was more out of place there than I was. And she had a tough time. She was part of a test exchange program, an attempt at bridging the gap between our two cultures. It was probably already too late for such things; the drought and rationing had already started before we even met. I think when we first became friends it was really because we had no other choice. No one else would have us. But it became a lot more than that. And so quickly."

Scout felt a sudden, startling pang. She had never given it a moment's thought, but hearing Ottilie say the word, Scout realized she had never really had any friends. Well, she had, back in the city when she was young. All dead now. But since then? She was friendly with people in the towns she worked in or traveled through. People who owned the food stands she frequented or flophouses she stayed in knew her on sight and were always happy to see her and swap stories. But that wasn't like having a friend.

As if sensing her thoughts, Shadow picked his nose up from the dusty floor to look back at her. Scout smiled back at him. Dogs totally counted as friends. And she and her friend had never been apart.

"We were at school together for six years and had plans to get a place together after. I was going to find a job; Ebba was going to keep studying, because at that time that was the only way a Space Farer could stay planetside. I mean, we always knew that our future was one of uncertainty and we couldn't really plan for more than a step at a time."

She stopped talking to examine a particularly elaborate mountain of loose junk, shining the light into every nook and cranny before continuing on. "We never did get that place. The war happened first."

"But you met up again after the war," Scout said. "That's a happy ending."

"I certainly thought so," Ottilie said with a humorless laugh. "For years and years, I thought so. That war, being apart for decades, not being able to see each other, growing older... Ebba still looks good, doesn't she? She looks just like she did the day I met her." She shined the flashlight over her scarred hands, the corded muscles of her forearms under the sun-damaged skin. "I didn't hold up as well. But she doesn't seem to mind."

"You can't let that Liv woman poison what you have with her words," Scout said. "She said some things to me too, secrets meant to hurt. She's crafty, like a fairy-tale character, knows just how much truth to tell to make you believe the lies."

"But Ebba admitted it."

"You know her heart."

"I thought I did." Her voice was raw with pain. She had let her anger go and it no longer masked her deep hurt. Scout desperately wished there was something she could do or say to help erase the last fifteen minutes of their lives. But there was nothing.

"I guess the only real question is, can you forgive her?" Scout asked. Her own feelings had changed. Ebba had seemed so kind, even to strangers, and yet it was entirely possible she had been part of the chain of command that had destroyed Scout's hometown and killed her family. Just the possibility, and she couldn't look at Ebba the same way. How much worse was it for Ottilie, who knew for certain just what Ebba had done?

"I have to," Ottilie said with a ragged sigh. "I don't think I have a choice. I don't have a life without Ebba. But I don't know how I can do it."

Scout realized the two of them had stopped searching, were just standing and talking as the dogs pulled at the end of their leashes, anxious to continue.

Then they started barking, both at once, like someone had flipped a switch from "calm" to "complete panic." Scout dug her heels in, gripping the leashes with both hands as the dogs jumped and pulled.

"What is it?" Ottilie asked, her voice all but lost in the chaos of dog noise. She shined her light all around, but neither of them could see what had set the dogs off.

"Wait!" Scout yelled. "Shine the light back up there!"

Ottilie took a moment to figure out what Scout was asking for. She had been passing the light over the hunched remains of a broken-down rover, but while moving it to the next pile of junk, she had briefly arced it up toward the ceiling far overhead. She put the light back up, deliberately, then found what Scout had only half seen.

A hatch in the ceiling hanging open, the bottom of a ladder just in sight. Ottilie moved to stand directly under it, shining the light up the long shaft.

"No one could jump up there from here," she said, loudly enough to be heard over the dogs.

"And the dust under it wasn't disturbed," Scout said. "But something spooked these two."

Ottilie kept shining the light around, her motions more and more jerky as the dogs kept barking and she kept not finding anything. Scout saw she had that object back in her hand, the one she had taken from the bag while Warrior went to confront Viola, the one she had quickly slipped out of sight when Viola had put her gun away. She spun back to Scout to hiss, "Get those dogs to quiet down!"

Scout reeled in the leashes until she had each dog by the collar and dropped down to one knee as she whispered calming nonsense. Shadow stopped barking first. His bark was more yip-like, shrill and annoying. Girl kept barking her deep, hellhound woofs, still too loud but not so painfully shrill.

Then Shadow was suddenly tense again, and Scout followed his line of sight to see Ebba approaching out of the dark. She was lurching about, hands waving in front of her, and Scout guessed her night vision wasn't up to the near-total darkness of this room. Her face was contorted in fear, but that fear faded into almost a smile as she finally met Scout's eyes, as if realizing she had succeeded in following the sound of barking to find the two of them.

Ottilie was facing the other way, shining the light up at the shaft. With Girl's continued barking, she had no idea Ebba was approaching.

"I think the top hatch on this thing is still open," Ottilie was saying. "I see the sky."

Ebba's still-waving hands brushed against Ottilie's back, just a whisper of fingertips over shoulder blade, but Ottilie was badly startled. She dropped the flashlight, and it spun away across the floor, lighting up mostly their legs in a series of flashes as if from a pulsar. Scout couldn't see what was happening, but she heard Ebba cry out, then saw her legs buckle and her knees go down into the dust.

"Ebba!" Scout cried, scrambling back to her feet.

"Ebba?" Ottilie said, dropping whatever was in her hand. Scout couldn't make out any details in the still-rotating light from the flashlight, just something the size of her palm, something flat on the side that had hit the ground and sharp spikes thrusting up into the air. Spikes that dripped with blood.

"What have you done?" Scout wailed. She wanted to rush forward, but so did the dogs. She held them back as Ebba, already on her knees, hands pressed to her belly, fell to one side. Ottilie lunged forward to catch her shoulders before her head hit the concrete.

"Ebba," Ottilie said again, pressing her own hand over Ebba's two. The blood gushed through all those fingers, unstoppable.

"Why?" Ebba said, more grief than pain marring her features. "I never meant..."

But she had no more words in her.

16

OTTILIE LET OUT a cry of such raw grief Scout felt tears spring to her own eyes.

She remembered her parents standing in the doorway to see her off, her baby brother bouncing up and down in her father's arms. She had stopped at the end of the street to look back one last time, certain they would have gone back inside to all the work that never ended inside the bakery, but they had been watching her still.

That had been her last glimpse of them: her mother's hand raised in a farewell salute, her father laughing as he pulled strands of his beard from her brother's sticky grasp. Her brother's baby giggles had echoed after her even as she turned to pedal away.

Ottilie's grief brought that all back, the sight but also the way the smell of baking bread had permeated the alley, the undertone of composting green matter from the bins that stood beside each doorway. She could even remember the distant feeling of the sun on her shoulders, muted by the dome above.

Scout was on her knees, no longer holding either leash. Shadow stayed close to her side, licking at her face as she fought back tears. Girl was sitting halfway between Scout and Ebba in Ottilie's arms, looking back and forth and thumping her tail uncertainly. She didn't know what to make of the mood in the air.

"Scout."

Scout jumped at the sound of her name, rubbing at her cheeks as she got back to her feet. Nothing there but Shadow's saliva, but still she felt ashamed. "She didn't mean to do it," Scout said as Warrior looked over at Ottilie rocking Ebba in her arms.

"Ebba let go of me in the dark," Warrior said. "Took me too long to notice she wasn't there. I doubled back, but couldn't find her. Were the dogs barking at her?"

"Not at first, I don't think so," Scout said, looking around for the fallen flashlight. It was some distance away, so instead, she just pointed into the darkness over Ottilie. "Do you see? There's a hatch."

Warrior moved to stand underneath it and Scout picked up the ends of the ropes and guided the dogs to the fallen light, but she stopped as a sudden thought hit her. "Is that safe?"

"Safe enough for me. You should probably stay back, though."

Scout stepped a leash-length back from both Warrior under the open hatch and Ottilie with Ebba in her arms.

"Did you see anyone?" Warrior asked, her head still tipped back to look up the shaft.

"No. No sign of footprints in the dust, either. But something had the dogs barking."

"That goes all the way to the surface," Warrior said.

"That's what Ottilie said."

Warrior looked down at Ottilie as if just then aware she was there. "We should take her back, get her calmed down. Get her to walk with you. I'll carry Ebba."

Scout put a hand on Ottilie's shoulder. She just buried her face into Ebba's neck and sobbed.

"Soldier," Warrior said sharply, and Ottilie stiffened but fell silent. "We need to move out." Then, more gently, "Let me carry her for you."

Ottilie sniffled once, then again, then sat back to lift Ebba up towards Warrior. She couldn't manage more than sitting the body up, but Warrior bent and took Ebba gently into her arms, rolling her close until her head was resting on Warrior's shoulder. Almost as if she was sleeping.

"Let's go," Warrior said, leading the way back across the hangar.

Scout waited for Ottilie to get to her feet. She stumbled back down twice, as if grief had made her drunk, and once she was standing she was far from steady, sort of leaning back and forth as she stared at the dust from the floor clinging to the sticky blood on her hands.

"We'll wash up inside," Scout said, putting both leashes as well as the light in one hand to grasp Ottilie by the elbow and guide her after Warrior.

"Why did she sneak up like that?" Ottilie asked.

"It was noisy, distracting," Scout said, but Ottilie didn't seem to hear her.

"She thought I did it on purpose, didn't she? When she was dying —what she said. She thought I was getting revenge. Didn't she?"

"I don't know what she thought," Scout said, but she had the sinking feeling that Ottilie was right. She was afraid Ottilie was about to collapse into tears again, but the older woman just nodded and let herself be led.

When they reached the locker room, they found Warrior had already laid Ebba out on one of the plastic benches and draped a long white towel over her, covering her face but not her feet. Scout could see the bulge where her hands were folded together over her stomach. The towel was slowly turning a brownish pink as it soaked up the blood. Scout steered Ottilie away from it, guiding her to the sinks.

"I think she's in shock," Scout whispered to Warrior as Ottilie dutifully washed her hands all the way up to the elbows.

"I think you're right," Warrior agreed.

"What happens if she snaps?"

"She's angry with herself. She won't snap and turn violent, if that's what you're worried about." But she wasn't looking at Ottilie, she was looking back toward the maintenance door.

"Should we block that with something?" Scout asked.

"No," Warrior said. "No need."

"But what if there is someone in there?"

"Then they have lots of ways to get into this part of the way station," Warrior said. "Through the parts Viola hasn't shown us. If there is someone out there, and they have been evading my detection, they can sure evade Viola's too. Blocking that door isn't going to stop them. In fact, I'd prefer if they do come after us that they use that door. That would be most convenient."

Ottilie turned off the faucet, then took a towel off the top of a stack on a shelf over the sink and began methodically drying her hands. Then she followed Warrior and Scout with the dogs back into the main room.

Clementine was sitting at the table drinking coffee from one of the bar mugs and eating one of the ready-made meals that had been scattered across the floor the night before. Scout couldn't tell which it was, just a tray filled with some sort of glop in a possibly tomato-based sauce. Clementine ate bite after bite with the deliberation of someone making a series of check marks on a to-do list.

Liv had moved her chair as close as possible to the doorway to the communications room and seemed to be trying to see the screens beyond. As she leaned forward, her elbow strayed too close to the doorway protection grid, and it glowed an amber warning until she sat back again.

"Viola up?" Warrior asked.

"Who knows? Couldn't find the Space Farer?" Liv asked.

"We found her," Ottilie said. She was looking at her own hands again, turning them over and over as if some speck of blood might still be there, nestled among the freckles and age spots.

"Where is she?" Liv asked.

"Dead," Warrior said, putting her hands on Ottilie's shoulders and steering her to a seat at the table, then going behind the bar for the bottle Viola had been drinking from the night before. She filled one of the mugs halfway, then crossed back to the samovar to top it off with coffee before pressing it into Ottilie's hands.

"It was an accident," Scout said, although whether she was talking to Ottilie or Liv, she wasn't quite sure.

"An accident," Liv repeated skeptically.

"We need to get Viola out here," Warrior said, looking at Ottilie slumped motionless over the mug for a long moment before lifting the mug to Ottilie's lips herself.

"She didn't leave us with a way to summon her, sadly," Liv said. She frowned in disgust as Ottilie sputtered over her swallow of coffee and liquor, letting it run down her chin to stain her jumpsuit. The little rivers of liquid traced snaky paths that seemed to deliberately avoid every spatter of Ebba's blood.

"What time is it, anyway?" Scout wondered. It felt like it was still night, but like it had been nighttime for eighteen hours at least. Disorienting.

"Three days and some change left sitting out this flare," Warrior said, then brought the mug back to Ottilie's lips. Ottilie was more alert this time, grasping the mug in her own hands to control what she swallowed. She set it back down with a deep sigh and Warrior left her alone with it, moving to stand behind Liv at the doorway.

"Are you going to deliberately set off an alarm?" Scout asked.

"If I have to. She can't hide away until we're gone, that's for sure."

"Why don't you use one of your clever gadgets to get us into the kitchen?" Liv asked. "We're nearly out of coffee, and I'd like something to eat besides a self-heating ready-made meal."

As if on cue, Clementine tore open another package, pulling the plastic strip out of the bottom of the tray to activate the heating element. The food inside began to bubble, the bubbling built to a crescendo, and Clementine split the top open and went back to shoveling food into her mouth, bite after bite.

"She sure does eat a lot for such a little thing," Warrior observed.

"You," Ottilie said, filling the sound with all her hate and rage. "This is your fault." She was still looking down at the mug clenched tightly in her hands, but then she lifted her head and fixed those steely eyes on Liv, who sat smirking in her hover chair.

"My fault?" Liv said.

"Yes, your fault. But I don't quite understand why. What do you gain from this?"

"Me? Nothing," Liv said with a shrug. "You are correct: I have nothing to gain, no motive, no reason at all to care about you or your lover. It does seem rather strange that it could be my fault, your little tiff."

Ottilie gripped the mug tighter still. Then she sighed, taking what was perhaps meant to be a calming breath, and drank down the rest of the contents of the mug in one long swallow.

Then she flung the mug at Liv with impressive accuracy. The stainless-steel mug toppled through the air end over end before striking Liv in the forehead with a sound like an ill-tuned bell.

"You stupid bitch, you ought to be thanking me," Liv growled, putting a hand to the red mark on her forehead. The stainless-steel mug didn't have enough weight to do any real damage, but Liv was directing her chair toward the table like she intended to run right over Ottilie, who was waiting for her with arms crossed and a look of challenge on her face.

"We have bigger problems," Warrior said. "Just sit quietly, both of you."

Liv relented, chin held high in smug superiority at being the master of her own emotions when Ottilie so clearly wasn't. She steered her chair to the farthest place at the table from Ottilie and parked there to watch what Warrior was going to do next.

"We should get in there, turn on all the lights, check all the cameras," Scout said, trying to see what was on the monitors without leaning into the doorway.

"Step back," Warrior said. "And hold your dogs."

Only then did Scout notice that Girl was growling again, an almost subsonic sound, but a persistent one. She was watching Clementine intently, and Clementine was staring right back at her. Scout caught Girl's collar and pulled her away, bringing her and Shadow back to the pallet they had slept on. Ottilie got up from the table and went to the bar, taking out another mug and half filling it from the bottle. Liv was watching her every move, that sardonic smile never leaving her face.

Scout had expected Warrior to produce another device from her belt to disable the systems protecting the doorway. But Warrior had a more low-tech approach in mind. She just raised an arm and stuck it into the communications room. The doorway flashed red and something popped. Then Warrior was falling flat onto her back, bolts of electricity dancing around her still-outthrust arm.

"You okay?" Scout asked when Warrior hadn't moved.

"Yeah," Warrior said, slowly lowering her arm. "Give me a minute."

"Did you take it down?" Scout asked, drawing nearer. The doorway looked just as blandly innocent as ever.

"No, I don't think so. But I bet I got Viola's attention."

Scout heard a bang, the sound of the hatch to Viola's private room being thrown back against the wall. She was stomping and cursing as she approached, kicking a fallen pillow out of her way as she crossed the barracks.

Then the sound of her curses was drowned out by a startled scream, and Scout turned to see Liv struggling with both arms to hold Ottilie's knife-wielding hand at bay.

17

WARRIOR PULLED her gun from its hiding place at the small of her back, but the dogs were faster. Shadow raised the alarm, leaping into the air over and over again, ever higher as he barked. But Girl went straight for Ottilie, tackling her and knocking her to the ground. The knife fell from her hand as she hit the floor, skittering away to disappear behind the bar.

"Get this dog off me!" Ottilie shouted.

"I don't know, maybe we should leave her there," Warrior said, putting her gun away. With all eyes on the knife fight and the dogs, Scout wasn't sure if the others had even seen it. "Scout, get the dog off her."

"Girl, come!" Scout said. Shadow responded first, trotting back to Scout's side to stand close to her calf. Girl looked back at him, then took her paws off Ottilie's chest to follow.

"Grab the knife," Warrior whispered to Scout, then put out a hand to help Ottilie to her feet. But she didn't let go once Ottilie was up. She hooked her foot around the leg of one of the chairs, spinning it around and pushing Ottilie back into it. She had both of Ottilie's wrists cuffed to the arms of the chair before Ottilie could even object.

"You can't do this. This isn't your jurisdiction," Ottilie said darkly.

"I'm not arresting you, I'm keeping you out of trouble," Warrior said.

"Then tie her up too," Ottilie said, pointing at Liv with her chin.

"What good would that do?" Scout asked. "It's not her hands that are the problem. It's her mouth. Why did you try to jump her, Ottilie?"

Ottilie didn't answer, just silently fumed. There was a red tinge to her cheeks that Scout could almost take for embarrassment. Ottilie struck Scout as someone largely driven by emotion and impulse, someone for whom stabbing was an appropriate response to Liv's whispered innuendos and provoking, "knowing" glances. But Warrior's reflective lenses were fixed on her now, and Scout knew just how that gaze felt, like being judged and found wanting.

It was nice to know it wasn't just Scout who felt like she didn't measure up.

"Knife, Scout," Warrior said, then turned as Viola finally passed through the doorway.

"I'm guessing you're the one trying to bust into my space. Anybody else would still be out cold," Viola growled at Warrior.

"Or dead?"

"No, not yet, but don't think I'm not considering cranking it up."

Scout found the knife under the shelving behind the bar and brought it back to Warrior.

"That's mine," Ottilie said, trying to twist her wrists out of her bonds.

"I'll give it back to you in three days," Warrior said. It wasn't a very large knife, more suited to paring an apple than murdering a grown woman. She tucked it into a pouch on her hip.

"Why was she trying to stab Liv?" Viola asked. "Did Liv kill Ruth?"

"No, she killed Ebba!" Ottilie said, trying to tuck her thumbs in tightly enough to slip her hands free.

"I'd sit still if I were you. Those are going to keep tightening if you struggle."

Ottilie looked down at her hands, which were already turning white from lack of blood flow, but she continued to twist and pull, shooting dark looks to first Warrior and then Liv.

"Ebba's dead?" Viola asked. "Ebba killed Ruth?"

"Ebba's death was an accident, and we still don't know who killed Ruth," Warrior said.

"But we think someone is creeping around in the hangar," Scout said to Viola.

"I doubt that," Viola said. "All the doors between there and the surface have been buried for decades."

"There's an air shaft to the surface," Warrior said.

"More than one," Viola said.

"One that's been left open."

Viola gave Warrior a disbelieving look but then relented, going back into the communications room to look at her monitors. "The solar particle detectors should have gone off," she mumbled to herself as she switched her screen through multiple monitor views so fast Scout didn't know how she could be taking any of it in.

"Can I come in?" Warrior asked.

"No," Viola said curtly.

"Look, I'm not going to be satisfied until I've scoured every centimeter of this place. You might as well just let me do it."

"I don't have to let you do anything," Viola shot back.

"You'd be wise to," Warrior said, unperturbed by Viola's growing bad temper.

"So, I have a question," Liv said conversationally.

"We can worry about coffee later," Warrior said over her shoulder.

"No, not that," Liv said. "This bottle here. I was noticing the brand."

"I noticed that myself," Ottilie said, finally sitting still.

Scout went back to the bar and picked up the bottle. "Star's End Bourbon," she said out loud.

Warrior shrugged and turned back to continue watching Viola.

"Star's End isn't a local brand. Although I can guess why you've heard of it," Liv said, the last directed at Ottilie.

"Space Farer bourbon?" Scout guessed.

"Goods have been moving through here since planetfall," Viola said. "That's a lot of war-free decades of unrestricted trade. Nothing strange about the occasional foreign origin of anything."

Scout turned the bottle over in her hands. "It says it was bottled ten years ago. That's right in wartime."

Viola scowled at her. "You want me to vent all the oxygen out of that room? Stay out of my business."

Scout quickly put the bottle down on the table, shooting a nervous glance to Warrior, but Warrior gave a small shake of her head. "It's an empty threat. This place is too porous for that. Although, to be fair, bottled ten years ago doesn't mean it came here right after. For all we know, she acquired it a week ago."

"No, I'm sure it was dropped from space during wartime," Liv said, steepling her fingers together under her chin. "Sounds like someone rewarded an informant."

"Shut your mouth," Viola grumbled, getting up from her chair to stand near the doorway.

"I don't think any of this is relevant," Warrior said with a frustrated sigh.

"Of course it's relevant," Liv said blithely. "Ruth was a spy, now she's dead. This woman is an informant, working with our enemies in the sky, and Ruth died in her home."

"I am not an informant," Viola said through gritted teeth.

"What could she inform on way out here?" Scout asked.

"Anything she can see with all that equipment," Liv said. "Equipment so old it's still tied into everything up above and down here. Does the planetary government even know this place exists?"

"Do they?" Ottilie pressed when Viola didn't answer.

"Someone must know somewhere. There are records," Viola said.

"Did you know when the asteroids were coming?" Scout asked. Viola flushed guiltily, but wouldn't meet Scout's eyes. "Did you know? Could you have warned people?"

"Not in time," Viola said, shoulders slumping. She passed through the doorway to where the bottle sat on the table. She picked it up, looking over the label as if it were all new to her. Then she set it back down without taking a drink. "There wouldn't have been enough time to evacuate everyone."

"You did know," Scout said. "You knew and said nothing."

"I couldn't have stopped it. The planetary government couldn't have stopped it, not even with the big guns. They just would have turned one big city-destroying rock into a shower of city-destroying debris."

"But people could have gotten out," Scout persisted.

"Not enough. There wasn't enough time! Don't you see? If I told the head of government, only those deemed the most important would have gotten away. They wouldn't have raised the alarm, just gotten their own people out and left the rest to die. I loathed that very idea."

"So? You could have told everyone."

"I'm telling you, most of them would have never gotten out in time. The cities weren't designed for evacuation. Those gateways out of the dome are too few and too narrow. People would have bottlenecked, panicked, died in terrible fear. At least without warning, it was a fast death."

"Fast," Ottilie said as if the word were bitter on her tongue.

"How much warning?" Scout asked. "Like, how many hours?"

"I don't know," Viola said, throwing her arms up in the air. "Most days I wasn't even watching. When I was… I don't know, an hour or two?"

Scout flopped down on the pallet, letting the dogs come close to each side of her. So it had been possible to know in advance. If Viola had known ahead of time, perhaps her father really had as well.

But why had he sent her away? Did he too worry that panicked people trying to flee the city would get bottlenecked in the gateways?

Why didn't he at least have her take her brother with?

"You should have been watching and warning," Liv said. "If you had all this information, why wouldn't you?"

"Because the first time I saw it, I realized I could only help the elite. And I chose not to. And after that, I stopped watching," Viola said. Her lips were pressed tightly together and her eyes were glassily bright, but she shed no tears.

"You never knew?" Scout asked Liv.

Liv looked horrified at that question. "Of course not!"

"Then my parents didn't know either?" Scout couldn't bear to look at anyone, just down at the dusty toes of her own boots as she waited for her answer.

"Honestly, I don't know. If they were who I think they were, you'd think they would've had a warning. Perhaps they had orders. Perhaps they could only get you out," Liv said.

"Oh, stop it," Warrior said, her voice so low it was nearly a growl. "You know nothing, you're just speculating. Stop messing with her head."

"She deserves to know the truth," Liv said with almost sincere innocence.

"Yes, she does," Warrior snapped, moving over to put a hand on Scout's shoulder. "Don't listen to her, kid. We talked about this before, remember?"

"But this would make so much more sense," Scout said, still looking at her own boots as she blinked back tears. "Just not being there when it happened for no reason at all. That makes no sense."

"Life frequently makes no sense," Warrior said. "And things happen for reasons that have nothing to do with most of us. A political squabble becomes a shooting war, and the side that's up in orbit deploys a horrifically nasty advantage on their enemy. For political reasons. Believe me, I've been over a goodly chunk of this galaxy and I can promise you, what seems like a reasonable action to a politician often makes no sense to the ones actually being hurt."

Scout nodded, for the moment still winning her own battle against the urge to break down in tears. She was functioning on too much coffee and too little sleep, but still. She wasn't a kid anymore.

"Kid, I'm sorry all this happened to you. It doesn't make sense to me either. But don't twist your memories of your parents to try to make sense of the unreasonable. Especially not to fit someone else's worldview. You'll find your own peace with it someday. And I know it sucks to hear 'be patient,' but that's all I've got."

"You don't know the first thing about the circumstances on this world," Liv said.

"I'm not fixing to learn about them by listening to you," Warrior said, the dangerous edge back in her voice. "You'll stop talking or I'll be gagging you. Am I understood?"

Liv pulled another face of exaggerated innocence, but nodded mutely.

"Good. Now Scout, come help me," Warrior said. Scout looked up at last to see Warrior in the communications room pushing buttons. She moved to join her, but Viola was faster.

"Don't touch that!" Viola snapped. "What are you doing?"

"Lights," Warrior said. "Cameras. Security feeds. I need to know if we're alone or not."

"That camera was on us in the main room," Liv said, her hover chair in the doorway as she pointed to one of the monitors, her vow of silence already forgotten. "Roll it back. Maybe we can find the poisoner."

"Later," Warrior said shortly, brushing aside Viola's hands as she tried to stop her from touching the equipment. "Just let me do this."

"I should have never let you all in here," Viola said.

"You couldn't have really kept us out," Warrior said. "Look at this, all these service shafts. Some of them are buried, but plenty of them aren't. It isn't remotely hard to get in here."

"Should we find a way to secure everything?" Scout asked. She leaned in as Warrior switched from camera view to camera view of empty hallways, dark rooms, Ebba under a blood-soaked towel. She was vaguely aware of Girl doing her subsonic growl again, of Viola and Liv crowding close behind her and Warrior, but she tuned it out, focusing on finding any sign of an intruder.

Her focus was shattered as the bottle fell from the table behind them and exploded into fragments of glass, the sound tinkling on after the first burst like whistling sparks falling from a firework.

Then the dogs were barking in real earnest.

18

"WHICH ONE OF THEM DID IT?" Viola asked, but Liv's chair was blocking the way for any of them to get back into the main room.

"Can't you shut those dogs up?" Liv demanded, then flinched back as Warrior lunged at her. But she wasn't attacking her, just hopping over the top of Liv's hover chair to run to Ottilie's side.

Scout had thought, as Viola apparently had, that one of the dogs had knocked the bottle to the floor, but that wasn't what had happened. The broken pieces were all around Ottilie's feet, Ottilie, who had been cuffed in a chair nowhere near the bottle on the table. But somehow she had gotten it, smashed it, and cut both her wrists to pieces trying to get out of the chair.

"Ottilie!" Warrior yelled, grasping the older woman's head and tipping it back to look into her face. Ottilie's lips worked like she was trying to form words, but nothing emerged. Scout squeezed between the front of the hover chair and the doorway to stand at Warrior's side. Ottilie's gaze moved from Warrior to Scout. She was pleading with her eyes, tears freely streaming as she struggled to speak. Warrior ripped off her own shirt to try to stop the bleeding, but Scout saw the life drain out of Ottilie's eyes.

"Why did she do this?" Viola asked as she and Liv drew nearer.

"Guilt," Liv said. "For killing her lover."

"No," Scout said. "She wouldn't have done this."

"She couldn't have done this," Warrior corrected, looking at the fragments of glass all around the chair. "She couldn't have reached that bottle."

"Maybe one of the dogs *did* knock it down," Viola said.

"Right into her?" Scout said skeptically.

"Anything is possible," Viola said.

"But not probable," Warrior said.

"Why couldn't she speak?" Scout asked. "She cut her wrists—why would that make her unable to talk?"

Warrior tipped Ottilie's head back again, gently opening her mouth, but there was nothing visibly wrong with it. Warrior's fingers probed every centimeter of Ottilie's skull, but in the end she just shook her head.

"An effect of the poison, maybe?" Scout wondered.

"We all had the antidote," Viola reminded her.

"Nobody could get in and out of here quick enough to do this," Warrior said, looking around the room.

Scout looked over at Clementine, who was halfway through yet another of the ready-made meals. She gave Scout a little smile between bites, a smile that didn't reach her eyes.

Warrior stood back up, wiping the blood from her hands on her own shirt. She looked suddenly tired, the skin around the lenses over her eyes drawn tight. She put a hand to the back of her neck and stretched.

"You liked her," Scout said.

"Respected her, I guess," Warrior said. "Come on, help me carry her to be with Ebba."

Scout helped Warrior cut the remains of the cord from around Ottilie's tattered wrists, then Warrior bent and lifted her out of the chair, throwing her over one shoulder and heading for the lockers. Scout followed behind with the bloody chair and Warrior's stained shirt. Warrior laid Ottilie on the bench next to Ebba's, folded her hands onto her belly in the same pose as her lover's, and draped another towel over her. Scout pressed a hand to her eyes, fighting back tears.

No one was loudly grieving, and she wasn't remembering her own loss, but seeing Ottilie there with no spark of life left in her felt like a great wrongness in the world.

To think, before she came here, she'd never seen a dead body. Now she'd seen three. And her heart pounded away, unable to slow back to normal.

She was terrified there would be more.

Scout took a deep breath and forced herself to drop her hand. "She didn't do this to herself," she said.

"No, she didn't," Warrior agreed, washing her hands in one of the sinks, then taking her shirt from Scout and soaping it up as well. "Liv seems very good at talking people into things. She's been trying to manipulate you since we got here."

"I'm not going to off myself."

"Ottilie didn't either," Warrior said. "As much as Liv may have wanted it, that's not what happened. I don't think that's what Liv wants out of you, anyway."

"Why would she want anything out of me? She doesn't even know me. And it's not like I have a fully equipped waystation or ties to the Space Farers. I'm just a messenger, a delivery girl."

Warrior turned the shirt over in her hands, finding another darkly stained patch to scrub at, but her head tipped as she glanced over at Scout. "Is that what you are?"

"Yeah," Scout said warily.

"Well, that's what you told me, and I have no reason to doubt you. But just as a general-purpose warning: You say you have nothing. Okay, I understand. You've lost your family. It's reasonable to feel that way. But given that, I would expect Liv to try to make you feel like you *do* have something. She needs you to believe that in order to manipulate you."

"What do you mean?" Scout asked.

"She can't convince a messenger and delivery girl that she ought to be helping Liv with whatever her game is. And believe me, she has a game," Warrior added. "But if she can convince you, you're really something else. Well."

Scout's scowl deepened. She didn't like where this conversation was going. She didn't have to search her mind long to find a different tack. "Everyone was right there with us, everyone except Clementine," Scout said, then bit her lip anxiously. Warrior just kept scrubbing at the shirt and Scout wondered if she had even heard.

"I think this increases the possibility that we aren't alone," she said at last, shaking out the shirt. The water droplets sprayed everywhere, but after four good thwacks, she slipped it back on. It wasn't as white as it had been, but it was quite dry.

"Clementine was right there with her," Scout said.

"I was watching out of the corner of my eye. I admit I looked away for a moment, but just a moment. I thought I saw something on one of the monitors… at any rate, it wasn't nearly enough time for Clementine to get up from the table, do that much damage, and sit back down again."

"It's more likely someone traveled from further outside the room and then disappeared again?" Scout asked.

"It's problematic," Warrior admitted. "I don't know what we're dealing with here. But do some investigative work on your own. Clementine doesn't have a drop of blood on her. If she did that to Ottilie, how'd she move so fast and stay so clean?"

Scout fell into a sullen silence. She could see the logic, but she couldn't bring her gut to believe it.

When they came back out into the main room, Liv was watching Clementine closely as she sipped at a mug and ignored the dog still intently growling at her. Scout shot Warrior a glance, and Warrior gave a conceding tip of her head, accepting Girl's perpetual distrust of Clementine as another piece of information, but not the conclusion. Scout sat down at the table where Ottilie and Ebba had sat the night before, eyes scouring every inch of Clementine even as her hand reached down to quiet the growling Girl.

Viola emerged from the kitchen with the samovar once more full of fresh coffee. She also had the last of the bread from the night before, some sort of nut paste darker than any Scout had tried before, and a little pot of honey. Scout's stomach rumbled loudly, and she eagerly reached for a piece.

"What happens now?" Viola asked, slumping into one of the chairs.

Warrior had gone behind the bar for more mugs. Someone had cleaned up the mess—glass, bourbon, blood, and all—leaving a large wet patch on the concrete floor. No one was sitting too close to that. Warrior filled a mug of coffee for herself and sat down between Viola and Scout.

"We need to conduct a search. We can work together on that," Warrior said, taking a sip of the hot coffee. The rich, roasted smell filled Scout's sinuses, hinting at the full alertness that was waiting for her. She gripped her pasted and honeyed bread between her teeth as she reached for a mug of her own. Liv gave her a disapproving look, but Scout didn't care about being unmannerly.

"I don't want to start poking around the whole place," Viola said. "I'm allergic to the dust."

"You sure leave a lot of it around for that to be the case," Liv said, wrinkling her nose as she looked around the room. And she hadn't even seen the state of the hangar.

"I leave it around because I flare up when I try to get rid of it," Viola snapped, rubbing at her temples as if Liv were giving her a headache.

"You don't have to poke around, I'll do that," Warrior said, taking another huge gulp of coffee as if the heat didn't bother her and the taste didn't interest her. She just needed to get the caffeine in her. "I want you on the cameras, in contact with me. If you don't have radios or comms, I have a work-around."

"I have comms," Viola said, looking around at the shelves as if she weren't quite sure where.

Scout took a cautious sip of the too-hot coffee, then quickly took a bite out of the crust of bread before the honey could drip onto the table. The dogs were watching her intently, anxious for any crumbs that might drop. Clementine was watching her just as closely, her hands folded neatly on her lap, as she had apparently finally finished eating.

"What?" Scout snapped at her. Viola and Warrior had pushed away from the table to find the comms and Liv was working the controls of her hover chair to follow them. Clementine didn't say anything, of course, just summoned another of those unconvincing smiles.

"What's your story?" Scout asked, moving her chair closer to Clementine. Girl gave a warning growl but was distracted by a corner of the bread that Scout tore off and dropped. She had to give another to Shadow before she could meet Clementine's blue eyes again. "I don't think Ruth knew the first thing about you. She was just room and board for you."

Clementine slowly blinked. But if that was meant to be an answer, Scout didn't know what that answer was.

"You're hardly the only war orphan wandering the streets of the cities. Most of us found jobs of one sort or another, helping out on farms or in factories, doing whatever little tasks we can until we're big enough for proper work. I've been biking messages and packages between the cities since the asteroid fell on my parents. If Ruth really was upset about the plight of all of us, why did she take just one of us in? Why not six, or eight? Why not do something actually helpful for all of us, or at least prompt her father to? A boarding school or something just to start. Why just acquire you like an accessory?"

Scout wasn't sure, but she thought the corners of Clementine's mouth were just beginning to crease, the start of a more genuine sort of smile.

Then Scout saw it: the light spray of blood that was still drying across the face of the cartoon character on Clementine's T-shirt. She leaned forward to get a better look, and Clementine recoiled, trying to cross her arms over herself.

She was going to obliterate the evidence! Scout leapt to her feet, catching Clementine's wrists in her hands and pulling them well away from her body. Clementine stumbled back, knocking her chair over and nearly striking Shadow with it. Scout let the momentum of Clementine's struggles pull her to her own feet. Scout was only a little bit taller, and Clementine was surprisingly strong given the bony spindliness of her arms.

"Scout!" Warrior commanded, and Clementine took advantage of Scout's momentary distraction to pull herself free. She straightened, giving Scout a look of pure victory, which lasted for all of a half of a second. Then she was on the ground, Girl's paws planted on her chest, the dog's snarling jaws closing on the girl's exposed neck.

## 19

"SCOUT!" Warrior shouted again.

"Girl, down!" Scout shouted louder still, and Girl looked up at her. Scout caught her collar to pull her off of Clementine, but it was too late. Her paws had wiped away every drop of blood.

"I expected better from you," Warrior said to Scout, extending a hand to help Clementine to her feet. "What'd you put in the coffee, testosterone?" she snapped at Viola.

"It's just coffee, and I've had more of it than any of you," Viola said. "You don't see me flipping out and attacking people."

"I wasn't attacking her," Scout said.

"Girl certainly did," Warrior said.

"Girl hasn't been drinking the coffee," Viola said.

"You said to investigate. I was investigating," Scout said. "She had blood on her shirt. It's gone now, but it was there. I was trying to keep her from wiping it away."

Warrior looked at Clementine, but the fine spray was quite gone. Ruth had clearly given her the best stain-resistant clothing if even blood could be simply wiped away.

"It was there," Scout said miserably.

"I believe you," Warrior said. "But Scout, she was closer to Ottilie than any of us. And those were arteries that were cut. Severed, to be more precise. It's not inconceivable that she got some on her quite innocently."

"Well, then, what?" Scout said, irritated to find herself once more blinking back tears. "If nobody can prove anything, then what?"

"Oh, I think one of us can prove something," Liv said, and her hover chair hummed closer. Apparently she had joined in the search for comms, but what she had instead was a small metal container, the sort used to store ammunition rounds.

"Was that in Ottilie's bag?" Scout asked. She had seen several similar containers in the rover, stacked around the table and in the unused bunk.

"No, it was just over there, under the blanket of dust," Liv said, hoisting it off her lap and onto the table. She grunted, laboring to move the container even with her well-muscled arms. Whatever was inside was quite heavy.

The color drained from Viola's face, but she just sank to the table, reaching for the coffee with a sigh.

"What is this, Viola?" Warrior asked.

"More of Liv's accusations," Viola said. "It's Space Farer credits."

"They deal in physical currency?" Warrior said, sliding back the lid of the container. Scout leaned in to see stacks of gold coins gleaming inside.

"Mostly for off-the-book payoffs," Liv said smugly.

"And quite useless here on the surface," Viola said. "This was nothing more than a symbolic gesture. It doesn't mean anything, just leave it alone."

Like Liv was ever going to do that. She looked over at Scout and raised an eyebrow, as if the two were sharing a moment. Scout just scowled. "The coins have dates stamped on them. Some of these are wartime vintage. Tell me, did you get paid to look away when the asteroids fell?"

Viola flushed a deep crimson.

"Enough," Warrior said wearily.

"All your talk of not being able to save the little people. This is blood money, isn't it, Viola?" Liv asked, her voice saccharine sweet.

"I said enough!" Warrior yelled. "You,"—she jabbed a finger at Liv —"stop talking. And you," she said, jabbing the finger in Viola's direction, "give me the codes for the door to the kitchen. We need something more calming than coffee."

"I'll fetch it," Viola said, getting up from the table. She hadn't yet defended herself from Liv's latest accusation, but her hands were shaking as she placed them on the table to push herself to her feet. She crossed to the kitchen door and appeared to whisper something to the wall. This doorway was not just protected by her security systems, it also had a heavy hatch she could slam shut and seal herself inside if she were so inclined. Warrior saw it too. She started to step through the doorway.

"No, the girls can get it," Warrior said, taking a seat at the table and motioning Viola to sit back down in the chair across from her. Liv was parked at the head of the table again, hands steepled as she watched the others move around her.

"I don't want to go in there with her," Scout said, glaring at Clementine.

"You're going to keep an eye on each other. Make us all some tea and find some soothing sort of snack. Girl can stay here with me," Warrior said, extending a hand to the dog until she crept over to sit at her side and keeping her there by feeding her little crumbs from the tabletop. Shadow followed Scout towards the kitchen. He didn't growl at Clementine, but he didn't take his wary eyes off her, either. "And take your time," Warrior added.

Scout paused to give a sharp nod, then followed Clementine into the kitchen.

Clementine opened all the cupboards, her gaze sweeping over all the contents before she started selecting items. Scout filled the kettle from the sink, watching Clementine out of the corner of her eye as the girl opened box after box of crackers, cookies, and hard biscuits, arranging a few of each into an elaborate pinwheel pattern on a large serving platter.

"Nice," Scout said, not as sarcastically as she had meant to. "This is the sort of skill one acquires when living with the governor's daughter, I suppose. High-level entertaining."

Clementine gave a little shrug, the closest Scout had yet seen her come to actually communicating. She carried on arranging her tray as Scout spooned loose-leaf tea into another samovar and waited for the kettle to come to a boil.

"So, these are gifts?" she heard Warrior asking in the other room.

"Yes, but not for me," Viola said. "I just gather them up when they fall from orbit and store them here."

"For whom?" Liv asked.

"For no one, really," Viola said.

Clementine caught Scout's eye and smirked, just a little uplift of one corner of her mouth. Scout gave a little nod; yes, Viola was being maddeningly evasive.

"Spill it, Viola," Warrior said, apparently thinking much the same.

"They were for my mother," Viola said in a rush. "She's been dead and gone for decades, happily married for decades before that. But when she was young, she went to the capital on a purchasing trip and met a Space Farer who fell for her hard. He never had a chance with her. She had already met my father, but that never stopped him from sending her all these gifts. The coins, the bourbon—anything here that's not from here is from him."

"Who is he?" Liv asked.

"I don't know," Viola said. "He signs the cards 'your lover who dwells above,' but I don't know his real name."

"He must be someone important to send such lavish gifts," Liv said.

"I gathered that much, thanks," Viola said sourly. "But I don't know how anyone becomes successful with such a loose grasp on reality. He has no means to know who even picks up what he drops or surely he'd know she's not even alive anymore to receive his gifts. I didn't even know about any of this until just before my mother died. My father was already gone, and I think she found it kind of romantic, having such a fervid admirer." Her voice had a warmer tone now, and Scout thought it was from remembering her mother, but Clementine rolled her eyes dramatically. Scout scowled at her again. How could she have such a lack of feeling? Didn't she remember her own mother?

The kettle finally beeped and Scout poured the boiling water over the loose tea in the samovar and shut the lid to let it steep, then picked up the heavy thing to carry back to the table. She realized she had turned her back on Clementine and hastily turned back, gesturing with her head for Clementine to move. Clementine picked up the tray and led the way back to the common room with an almost cheerful spring to her step.

What was she playing at now? No more grief for her adopted mother, not even a day dead. Strange girl.

Scout set the samovar down on the table and took a seat next to Warrior. Liv had a stack of notes spread across the table in front of her. Scout recognized the square gray card stock and the harsh red lines of the most common font the Space Farers used. Scout reached across to grab a few of the cards. The messages were short, just rather benign well-wishes, each signed

"from your lover who dwells above."

"Pretty tame for a fervid secret admirer," Liv said, holding one up for Viola to see. Viola ignored her, reaching for one of the richer, butterier cookies on the tray. Her thick fingers scattered Clementine's careful arrangement, but the girl didn't seem to mind. She had sat down at the end of the table opposite Liv and was watching them all with a dreamy smile on her face.

Liv put the cards in groups, then examined the messages and arranged them into different groups. Then she sat back, still frowning.

"What are you doing?" Scout asked.

"There must be a pattern," she said. "There's no passion here, just words. This must be a different sort of communication, not one of the heart. But definitely secret."

"What do you mean?" Scout asked.

"A code, my dear child," Liv said, leaning forward to change her groupings.

"There's no code here," Viola said. "He's a gentleman, is all. Not everyone needs turgid passion in their lives."

"Case in point?" Liv asked, raising an eyebrow at Viola.

"I'm perfectly happy living alone," Viola said grumpily, then reached for another cookie, holding it between her teeth as she poured herself a mug of tea from the samovar.

"It does seem a bit farfetched," Warrior said to Liv.

"Perhaps you're right," Liv said, tapping her fingertips on the table as she regarded yet another arrangement of the cards. "Perhaps it's something much simpler. Baser."

"What are you on about now?" Viola asked, her mouth full of cookie. She washed it down with a long gulp of tea and seemed to enjoy Liv's wincing at her manners.

Liv took a deep breath, not quite rolling her eyes, as if her point should be perfectly obvious and they were all being dense. "Your mother met this fellow shortly before you were born?" Viola nodded, eyes narrowing in growing suspicion.

"Drop this," Warrior said, her voice a low growl, but Liv ignored her.

"Isn't it obvious? The reason this 'secret admirer' would keep sending gifts, even though your mother is dead and gone?" Liv asked, all false sweetness again. "They were never for her, or not just her. They were for you. After all, she was just a woman he had known for a brief moment, but you—you're something more."

Viola put down her mug, her face once more darkening. She narrowed her eyes even further, leaning forward as if she were about to spit something out. Maybe a carefully chosen word, maybe a venomous spray, like a lizard. But nothing passed her lips.

"You're his daughter, my dear," Liv said, quite needlessly. Scout was certain even the dogs had picked up what she was driving at. Liv just smiled at Viola, her faux concern undermined by the glee in her eyes as she waited for Viola to explode.

And explode she did, her whole body spasming before she spewed tea, cookie bits, and hot, scarlet blood over all of them.

## 20

WARRIOR LUNGED ACROSS THE TABLE, catching Viola's arm but seeming not to know what to do. Viola looked up at her, her eyes wide with fright. Like Ottilie, she struggled to speak, fingers clawing at her throat, but she couldn't get a word out or even draw breath. Warrior caught her head before it fell to the table, only to gently set it down. Viola was dead.

There was a quiet moment, then a clatter as Liv's tea mug fell from her numb fingers. She looked at them each in turn, her piercing eyes searching for signs of guilt. Then she put two fingers in her throat and attempted to make herself vomit.

Warrior was still standing with one knee on the table, her hand on the back of Viola's head. She looked over at Liv. "That likely won't work. Where did that antidote gun go?"

Liv was dry heaving, but managed to bring up the little bit of tea she had drunk.

"The tea wasn't poisoned. I made the tea," Scout said. "It was the cookies. Clementine brought the cookies."

Clementine shook her head vigorously, her eyes round as if shocked to be accused.

"You know you did!" Scout said. "I only turned my back on you for a second, not even a full second. How did you do it?"

Clementine shook her head again, tears glistening in her eyes, all hurt betrayal as if Scout were her best friend for life and had inexplicably turned on her.

"This is insane," Warrior said. "Just four days to wait out the storm. Why is that so hard? Why can't you people just keep from killing each other?"

"There's just one killer here," Scout said, pointing at Clementine.

"Don't be ridiculous, she's just a little kid," Liv said, wiping bile from her lips onto the back of her hand.

"And we know she didn't kill Ebba," Warrior said. She was still half on the table, her reflective lenses moving from Scout to Clementine and back. "Well, there's nothing else for it. Everyone get in a chair."

"I assume you don't mean me. I'm already in a chair," Liv said calmly.

Warrior seemed to think about it. "No, you'll be fine as you are. Set your hands on the arms of the chair, well back from the controls."

"Why?" Liv asked.

"Because I no longer trust any of you," Warrior said, reaching for the pouch on the side of her belt where she kept her thin cuffs, just like the ones that had kept tightening around Ottilie's wrists.

"What makes you think any of us trust you?" Liv asked.

"I'm an officer of the law. Not local, but still."

"You could be anybody," Liv said, reaching for the control to back up her chair.

"But I'm not anybody," Warrior said, snatching Liv's wrist and cuffing it to the arm of the chair in one swift motion. She then caught her other hand and did the same. Then she pulled something from the back of her belt and showed it to Liv. "My badge."

Liv leaned forward to examine what Warrior was showing her. Then she sat back again, turning her head away and raising her chin. But if she thought the badge was inauthentic, she said nothing.

Warrior turned to the other two, another set of cuffs in her hand. Clementine was sitting primly in her chair, her hands already resting on the arms. She remained motionless as Warrior cuffed her to the chair.

"Make sure they're tight," Scout said. "I don't trust her."

"They're tight," Warrior said.

"Are you sure? She's quite small."

"They're tight," Warrior said again. "You, come with me."

"I thought we were all going to be cuffed in here," Liv said.

"I'm separating these two," Warrior said, putting a hand on Scout's shoulder to steer her into the communications room.

"Maybe I don't want to be left alone with this one," Liv said.

"So you think she's dangerous, too?" Warrior asked.

"I don't know what to think anymore," Liv said. Her head was down, the hair that had worked loose from her tight ponytail obscuring her face. Scout wanted to step closer, to see if the weary despair in Liv's voice was real. But Warrior's hand tightened on her shoulder, and she continued on into the communications room.

"That chair there," Warrior said. Scout sat where she had pointed, putting her hands on the armrests and allowing herself to be cuffed. Warrior didn't draw the cuffs tight, but then she didn't need to. Scout was sure if she tried to twist her way out of them, they would tighten up on her.

Warrior turned to the bank of monitors, cycling through all the camera feeds. There was nothing to be seen. The cameras posted outside were fuzzy with interference from the particle storm. Proof enough that the solar event was still going strong. Warrior looked over the controls, found the switch she was looking for, and turned the lights on inside the hangar. Several of the screens around her that had been opaque flared to life, showing various views of the mountains of trash inside the hangar. Nothing was moving.

Warrior frowned, rubbed a thumb along her chin, and leaned over the controls again, hands flying as she summoned windows of text and changed values in the settings, then switched to the next window before Scout could quite read anything.

"What are you doing?" she asked.

"Changing some of Viola's parameters," Warrior said, fingers not slowing. "The cameras have motion detectors. I'm assuming she had the sensors set the way she did to avoid her cat setting things off, but I'm jacking up the sensitivity. If the smallest mouse stirs, I want a warning."

There were a lot of cameras, a lot of settings to be modified. Scout quickly grew bored with the screens of text she couldn't see from across the room. But, unlike the chairs in the common room, the chair Scout was cuffed to could pivot. With nothing happening on the monitors, she turned to the side to see what they were doing in the common room. Liv didn't appear to be talking, but with her head down and her face covered by her hair, it was difficult to be sure. Clementine sat perfectly still, as if they were having some sort of game of who could be the quietest. The smile curving her lips said she was certain she was winning.

"Should we be asking her questions?" she asked Warrior.

"Hmm?" Warrior said absentmindedly.

"Clementine," Scout said. "Why does she keep killing people?"

"How is she going to answer?" Warrior asked.

"She can talk," Scout said darkly, although she wasn't sure that was true.

"If she's as skilled at being an assassin as you seem to think she is, neither of us would ever get her to talk," Warrior said. "I'm almost more worried about leaving her alone in there with Liv. But I guess Liv is only dangerous when she talks."

"I don't think she's talking now," Scout said.

"No, she isn't," Warrior said.

"How much of you is real?" Scout asked.

"How much of me is real?" Warrior repeated, surprised.

"I mean, you have those nanites. Those are weird. They do what— fight infections, poison, protect you from solar particles—"

"Where I come from, they aren't that unusual," Warrior said.

"Do lots of people have them, or just officers of the law?" Scout asked.

"Lots of people," Warrior said. She had finished adjusting all the camera settings and was sitting back in her chair, arms crossed as she studied all the monitors. But nothing was happening.

"And your eyes," Scout went on. "You can see in the dark. You can see those gadgets when the screens aren't even showing anything or what they show doesn't make any sense to me. Is that normal?"

"No, that's pretty much just for officers of the law. At least for now."

"I suppose it's expensive," Scout said.

"Body modifications are always expensive," Warrior said.

"So someone like me wouldn't be able to get any of that," Scout said.

Warrior swiveled in her seat to look at Scout. "Would you be interested in that sort of thing?"

"The hardware or the job?" Scout asked.

"Well, both," Warrior said.

"I don't know," Scout said. "I always assumed I would always be here."

"Why is that?" Warrior asked.

"I don't know," Scout said again.

"I think you're old enough to start thinking about these sorts of things," Warrior said. "It's a big universe."

"Yeah," Scout said. "I guess so."

"Listen," Warrior said, turning to face Scout and leaning forward to rest her elbows on her knees. "The universe is full of kids like you. Kids that just sort of get stuck. I've seen it a thousand times, but it never stops making me feel heartsick."

"What do you mean?"

"Your family is gone. This job of yours can't be that thrilling. I guess you stick with it because it keeps you out here in the wild most of the time. I know you're mostly waiting around for the rebels to discover you, but I promise you that's no real life, either."

"How do you know what I'm doing?" Scout asked.

"Come on, kid. You know I'm right."

"So what? You act like I'm stuck because I choose to be stuck."

"Aren't you?"

"No. Say I wanted to leave—how would I even do that? Especially now, with the war about to start up again. There is no path for someone like me to get off this planet."

"See, that's where you're wrong," Warrior said, turning back to the banks of monitors. "There's always a way, if you're clever."

"I am clever," Scout said. "I've been on my own for years. I wouldn't have made it this far if I weren't clever."

"All right, perhaps the question is: Are you clever enough?"

"If I wanted to leave, would you take me?" Scout asked, her voice softer than she would have liked. She drew herself up taller in the chair to compensate.

"Do you want to leave?"

"Why wouldn't I?" Scout asked. Such a strange question after how hard Warrior had been selling life in the universe at large.

"Because out there, you'd be no one special."

"I'm no one special here," Scout said.

"Aren't you? All of this analyzing coincidences you keep doing? Isn't that because you think you *are* special?"

"What do you mean?"

"Deep down, don't you want to believe that your parents were spies? That they got you out of the city in time for some grand reason? That the rebels are waiting for the perfect moment to bring you into their fold, maybe even make you their leader?"

Scout scoffed.

"If you stayed here, you could wait forever," Warrior went on, "always sure that the next day would be *the* day. The day you would find out what it all meant, why you weren't there when your family died. Why you were spared when they were not. But if you go with me," Warrior said, looking back over her shoulder at Scout, "you'll have to admit there was no reason."

"That it was random?"

"That it doesn't matter why. It doesn't affect you. Obviously, the *event* affected you; I'm not saying you're wrong to grieve your family. But trying to find out why isn't helpful. Because in the end, that reason doesn't matter. Not in regard to what you do with the rest of your life, not in regard to who you are. You'll have to give up the idea that there was a reason you survived, and they didn't. The idea that you can build your life around that reason. Because there is no reason."

"Then what?" Scout asked.

"What do you build your life around?" Warrior asked. "Listen, they didn't die so that you could do something great with your life. They didn't sacrifice themselves for you. They just died. But you can do something great with your life to show that it matters that you did live when they didn't. Do you see the difference?"

"Maybe," Scout said slowly. "I have to think about it."

"Good answer," Warrior said, turning back to the computers.

Girl peeked her head into the communications room. Slowly, she padded up to sit next to Scout's feet. Then she put one enormous paw on Scout's knee. Shadow was watching from the doorway.

"I think they need to go again," Scout said. "Can you take them to their spot in the bathroom?"

"Tell you what," Warrior said, getting up from her chair and pulling Ottilie's little knife from the pouch on her belt. "I'll cut you free. You can take them yourself."

"So I'm among the trusted again?" Scout asked.

"Kid, you never left. Go on, let your dogs do their business. When you get back, you're going to help me search the complex. The cameras aren't sensing anything, but I still don't think we're alone."

"Got it," Scout said as Warrior snipped the cuffs away.

"She's free while the rest of us are still tied up?" Liv said as Scout passed through the common room, guiding the dogs to the bathroom.

"I can keep an eye on one of you loose at a time, and she goes first because she's the one with the dogs," Warrior said. "If I'm right and we're not alone, watchdogs are going to come in very handy."

Liv had something else to say, of course, but Scout tuned it out as she passed through the storage room to the bathroom. She waited for the dogs to finish, then cleaned up when they were done. She took a moment to herself, trying not to think of the bodies laid out on the benches in the back corner of the room. Ruth's body was still in the barracks, and no one had bothered to move Viola from where she'd fallen on the floor in the common room. It didn't seem right. She should tell Warrior that they should do something with it.

When she was done washing her hands, she whistled the dogs to her side and headed back to the common room. At first it looked like Warrior was reaching inside Liv's hover chair to cut her bonds. Scout was a little annoyed at how easily Liv had talked her way out of being tied up. But then she realized the jerky motions Warrior was making were nothing like the smooth motions of clipping off a cuff. The two of them were fighting over something.

The chair lurched, then both their hands were grappling up into the air, and Scout saw it: Warrior's gun. Warrior must have been setting Liv free, and Liv had made a snatch for the gun.

Scout ran into the common room, the dogs close at her heels. "Why did you cut her free?"

"I didn't," Warrior said, pivoting her weight to drive her elbow into Liv's jaw. Liv cried out, and Warrior took two steps back, the gun now firmly back in her own hands. But before Scout could take a breath of relief, Warrior's whole body went rigid. The gun clattered to the floor. Warrior fell to her knees, then flat on her face. There was a tiny tinkling sound.

Scout looked at the small patch of blood in the center of Warrior's back, the rapidly growing patch of blood. Then she looked up to see Clementine standing over Warrior's body, Ottilie's little knife in her hand, blood dripping from the blade onto the toes of her canvas shoes.

Clementine smiled.

## 21

SCOUT FELT a moment of panic as the dogs charged at Clementine. It didn't look like much of a knife, but it had been enough to take down Warrior. The dogs had no fear of it. But Clementine made no move to defend herself as the dogs jumped on top of her. The knife went skittering across the floor to disappear under one of the shelves. Girl and Shadow were both on Clementine, and the girl tucked her head in her arms close to her chest, drawing up her legs to curl into a ball. The dogs were probably biting her, but Scout couldn't muster the empathy to care.

Liv said nothing, her eyes inscrutable as she watched the girl try to crawl toward the table. Instead Liv drew closer to where Scout still stood motionless, Warrior sprawled at her feet.

Then Scout finally dropped to her knees at Warrior's side. The blood was spreading everywhere—so much blood for such a little cut.

"What is she?" Liv asked.

At first, Scout didn't understand the question. Then she saw the sparks erupting from Warrior's knife wound. It looked like Clementine had been aiming for her kidney, but had hit something quite different.

Scout turned Warrior over and pulled her into her arms. Warrior looked up at her, really looked up at her. Scout realized the tinkling sound she heard when Warrior fell had been one of her lenses shattering against the floor. Now one blue eye was looking up at her from between the jagged edges of the broken lens still clinging to her cheek. The other lens was scratched but intact. The effect was disconcerting.

"Scout," Warrior said, her hand clutching Scout's arm.

"You can heal from this, right?" Scout asked, wanting to press her hand to stop the flow of blood, but worried what those sparks meant.

"Not this time, kid," Warrior said.

"Oh, no… the cat. You gave your nanite to the cat," Scout said. "It's all my fault."

"One nanite wouldn't have made any difference," Warrior said. "I can heal from almost anything, but not a direct hit to my power source. I'm draining away."

"No—there must be something we can do," Scout said, looking back over her shoulder to the closed hatch that led to Viola's room.

"No time," Warrior said, the hand on Scout's arm squeezing weakly. "Listen, kid. Remember what we talked about. You said you were clever; you're going to have to be more than clever to get off this planet. But don't stay here. This isn't the place for you."

"You were going to take me with you," Scout said. Not a question.

"I was going to take you with me," Warrior agreed. Her fingers clutched one last time, then behind the broken lens the blue eye that was looking at her rolled back and Scout knew she was gone.

Scout laid her gently on the floor, then picked up Warrior's fallen gun and tucked it into the waistband of her cargo shorts. Her fingers felt numb; her whole body felt numb. She didn't feel like she was really there, more like she was watching herself move from a great distance away. Like she was watching herself the way she had watched Warrior when she first left the rover. A remote, untethered sort of feeling.

She knew it well. She had felt the same that day when the asteroid fell, and for days after. Her emotions would catch up with her soon enough, but for now she would just keep moving, keep doing all the necessary things in complete dispassion.

The gun tucked away, she turned back to the others. Clementine was sitting on the table, knees drawn up to her chest to keep her feet out of reach of the dogs.

Liv had disappeared. Scout couldn't manage any feeling of surprise. She just turned to Clementine. With Warrior gone, there was no one left to convince her not to ask her questions.

"You knew," Scout said. "You knew exactly where to hit her. Clearly you want us all dead. I have no idea why. Not sure I care. But I do wonder: Why am I still alive?"

Clementine stood up on the table, towering over Scout. The smile was gone, a welcome change, but her placid face revealed nothing of her thoughts.

Scout looked around until she found the knife under the shelves. Keeping one eye on Clementine, she reached under the shelving to fetch the blade and put it in her back pocket next to her own utility knife. She still had her slingshot, and, of course, Warrior's gun.

She wasn't sure it would be enough.

"I know you understand me. You might not be able to talk, but if you wanted to, you could communicate with me. You could answer all my questions. You *choose* not to," Scout said.

Clementine just shrugged.

"Are we alone here? The two of us and Liv?"

Clementine shrugged again.

"Are you going to be killing us, too? Why wait? Why didn't you just poison us all the first night?"

Another shrug.

Warrior had said that she hadn't untied Liv, and yet Liv and Clementine had both been freed. Had one escaped and uncuffed the other? Were they working together? "Is Liv in on it with you? Where is she now? What is she going to do?"

Clementine sighed. She gave Scout a long-suffering look, as if she didn't mind the questions so much as being asked all the wrong questions. Well, those were the only questions Scout knew. She guessed Warrior had been right that it was futile to ask.

"Whatever. I'm going to check the monitors." Scout went into the communications room, walking sideways to keep one eye on Clementine, still standing on the table. The dogs stayed near the table, Girl making her customary low growling sound that built in intensity every time Clementine moved a centimeter.

Scout looked at all the screens. She saw Liv moving through the hangar, hugging the wall, but still visible on all the cameras. Scout didn't know where she was heading, or if she even knew where she was heading. Did she have a master plan, or was she just looking for somewhere to hide in her chair until the storm had passed? Scout called up a schematic of the entire station and looked for anything interesting in the direction Liv was headed.

Suddenly, both of the dogs were barking like mad. Scout pulled the gun from her waistband and charged back into the common room. Clementine was still standing on the table, but she had something in her hand. She opened her fingers to show it to Scout. It was a palm-sized cylinder with a red flashing light on one end. She smiled that maddening smile again, then tossed the cylinder to Scout.

Scout flinched away, covering her face with her arm without lowering the gun. The cylinder made a small popping sound, and the air filled with a thick smoke. Coughing, Scout rushed up to the table, but Clementine was gone. The dogs were still barking, half in panic now. They didn't like the smoke.

"Come, dogs!" Scout commanded. The two dogs came to her side and followed her into the kitchen. The kitchen had a hatch, a door she could shut and lock from the inside. She slammed it shut and bolted it, then found a large tray to dissipate what little gas had flowed in from the other room.

If only the communications room had had a door. Being able to see all over the station would've been nice. But the kitchen was probably better. She didn't think the hatch would be impenetrable, but she was sure that anyone trying to get in would make a great deal of noise. Enough to wake her if she should fall asleep. Certainly enough to wake the dogs. This was as close as she was going to get to safe for now.

Surely she and the dogs could wait out the storm here. They had food, they had water, they could make do with the plumbing. Just three more days.

But *was* she safe? Was there another door?

Scout went into the pantry where she had seen Liv and Clementine speaking before that first dinner. The room was lined with shelves filled with more MREs, as well as cans and packages of food she could cook. That would probably come in handy; whatever had killed Viola could be in any of the food in the kitchen. She hadn't turned her back on Clementine long enough for her to poison that tray of food, she was sure of it. Clementine must have poisoned everything that first night. Scout would be sticking to food she could clearly see hadn't been tampered with, food that would reassure her with the soft hiss of released vacuum compression when she opened it.

The pantry wasn't large, and there was no second door. She looked up at the camera over the doorway. It was possible either Liv or Clementine could be watching her on the monitors in the communication room. But Scout didn't think that would matter. Once they entered the common room and saw the locked hatch to the kitchen, they would know where she had gone.

Scout looked at the refrigerator that had been calling to her since she had first arrived. Row after row of gleaming bottles of jolo. More than she could drink in a week. Each individually sealed. Safe. And the last thing she wanted now was sleep.

Scout took out a single bottle of jolo and closed the fridge door, then changed her mind and fetched a second. She brought them both to a heavy chopping block that sat directly across from the hatch. She sat on the floor with her back to the block, the dogs settling in on either side of her. She set the second bottle behind her on the block and turned the first bottle over in her hands.

She didn't really want it. Not like she had before. She was still numb; this apathy was part of that. She thought of Warrior with her broken lenses, lying on the floor in arm's reach of Viola's body. Their blood pooling over the floor was probably flowing together by now. Scout remembered that blue eye. She had imagined voids of darkness behind those lenses, but never eyes like those. The same intense shade of indigo the sky had been the day her family died.

Scout sighed, still handling the bottle without quite opening it. Even her most morose thoughts weren't bringing the tears. She would just have to live with the numbness until it was gone. Perhaps it was better this way. Clementine would surely be back, and Scout didn't want to be caught crying when she needed to be fighting.

She needed to be alert. She needed the caffeine and the sugar. She had to drink the jolo.

She wiped nonexistent dust from the neck of the bottle before finally popping it open and taking a long swallow of icy cold fizzy goodness. Her brain sang at the sweet rush of sugar, if a bit more muted than its usual opera to the glories of jolo.

Just three more days.

22

THE BUZZ from the sugar and caffeine made for a very different sort of numbness. Scout sipped slowly at each bottle, not really aware of how much time was passing beyond the count of the empties she lined up against the wall. After ten bottles, she felt like she really ought to eat something—her hands were shaking from all the caffeine—but she was too tired to get up and find food.

She had gotten up earlier to give each of the dogs an MRE's worth of beef stroganoff. They had licked the trays clean, but as per usual with dogs, they had pushed the trays all across the floor while accomplishing that. One was in the corner near the empty jolo bottles, but the other had slipped under one of the ovens, and from time to time one or the other of the dogs would sniff under the oven, smelling that last bit of rich gravy they couldn't quite reach. Scout was sure it was maddening, but couldn't work up enough interest to get up and retrieve it for them.

She had just popped open an eleventh bottle and brought it to her lips when the lights went out. There was a long moment in total darkness, then a red light appeared over the doorway between the kitchen and the pantry. There was another red light on the other side, Scout could tell from the pattern of the inky shadows. She stood up and crossed to the hatch, trying to listen through the door.

At first, it seemed far too thick to hear anything, and Scout's hand moved to the bolt to open the hatch enough to peek out. Then she heard a crash, followed by more crashes, then complete silence.

Scout strained her ears to hear more—a voice, footsteps, anything— but the silence stretched on for minute after minute. At last she could take it no more. She slid the bolt back as quietly as she could, then turned the wheel until the hatch swung ever so slightly ajar.

"Come, dogs," she whispered, pointing at her side. Shadow was there in an instant, but Girl was still cowering next to the chopping block. Scout let the door swing open anyway, stepping back a bit in case anyone was about to charge inside. But there was no one there.

The common room was also lit by red emergency lights. There was a burnt smell in the air that made Shadow sniffle, then whine. Scout thought at first that it was the remains of the smoke grenade, but it was too strong for that. She crossed the floor to where Warrior still lay on her side and knelt to take the light from Warrior's belt. She shined it around the room, but there was no sign of anyone there besides her and Shadow, and now Girl hovering in the kitchen doorway.

But there was smoke curling in from the communications room.

Scout started to rise but then knelt back down again. She was going to need more than a light. And she was sure Warrior would want her to have whatever she needed. Especially if the alternative was Liv or Clementine having it. Scout took a deep breath, pushing back the voice in her head that said she was only telling herself what she wanted to hear, and reached for the clasp on Warrior's belt to snap it open. It took a moment to get it out from under Warrior's hips; she had forgotten just how heavy Warrior was.

When it was at last free, she belted it around her own waist. At first it hung too low on her hips, threatening to slip down to the ground around her feet, but then it started tightening, much like the cuffs had done around Ottilie's wrists. Scout pulled the gun from her waistband as the belt settled around her waist, then tucked it into its holster at the back of the belt.

She looked down at Warrior's still face. The broken lens was probably useless, but she might end up needing the other. She touched the edge of it, worried that she was going to have to claw it free, to dig into Warrior's face with her nails, but it popped free at the first brush of her fingertips and she slipped it into one of the belt's many pouches.

Light in hand, one loyal dog at her heels, she crept up to the communications room. The smell was definitely from an electrical fire, the noxious odor of melted circuit boards and wires. She saw the legs of one of the chairs thrusting out from the bank of monitors toward the center of the room, then saw where the seat was embedded among the smashed screens. Not a single screen was unharmed. But this wasn't why the lights were off, Scout was sure. Why would either Liv or Clementine cut the lights, then stand here silently for so long before destroying the equipment? It made more sense that the electricity had been cut to the entire station from somewhere else, then whichever one of them had done it had walked or hovered here to make sure no one could get a signal out even if they restored the power.

There must be another place from where someone could control the power. A utility room of some sort.

Scout gasped aloud as a horrible idea struck her. Was the airflow off too? She looked around, found a vent, and put a hand in front of it. She could feel a faint stirring of the air and breathed a sigh of relief. It made sense; the emergency lights were on, there must also be emergency power to the air systems. Still, she wanted everything back on as soon as possible.

But where could a utility room be?

That could have been where Liv was heading when she traversed the hangar. In fact, the only other door Scout hadn't gone through was the one on the other side of the barracks, the one to Viola's private space.

Scout signaled for Shadow to follow her as she pressed on, past the communications room to the barracks. Girl whined for a moment, then ran to catch up, not wanting them out of her sight. Shadow glanced back at her, then turned his focus back to the corridor between the bunks. This room also was empty, save for Ruth's corpse wrapped in a sheet in the bunk under where Scout had tried so briefly to sleep.

The only other way out was the hatch to Viola's rooms. Scout wasn't sure if it would be locked or not. There was a panel next to the door, the sort that controlled locks and room climate in the nicer places Scout had been. It was unsmashed but completely dark. Scout grabbed the handle on the door and gave it a push. It swung open, and she stepped over a threshold into a small sitting room, just two chairs on either side of the hatch turned to face each other. Next to one was a basket filled with balls of wool and an assortment of knitting needles. Next to the other was a table that held a cup and saucer half filled with a brown liquid that smelled like tea.

It only took two steps to cross the room through another open hatch to a room dominated by a large, poufy bed. Perhaps the mattress was hard as a rock, but the comforters piled on top of it were each puffier than the last, and Scout had no idea what any one person could even do with such an enormous number of pillows. There wasn't room enough to step inside without climbing up onto that bed. Definitely no room for anyone to be hiding, although she poked at the pile of comforters just to be sure.

Then something mewed. Girl immediately began making her I-want-to-play-with-that whining noise, wagging her tail furiously as she attempted to force herself between Scout and Shadow and charge into the room to find the mewler.

"Girl, stay!" Scout said, grabbing her collar to pull her back. "Stay!"

Shadow sat down in his best erect posture like a soldier at parade rest, but Girl just kept squirming.

Scout leaned into the room and found the cat tucked between the foot of a bed and the side of the room opposite where the open door stood. He looked up at Scout, tail flicking imperiously back and forth as he regarded her.

"You're probably fine where you are, Tubbins," Scout said to the cat. "We'll leave you be."

She was about to lean back out of the room when something caught her eye. Something was resting on a little shelf over the head of the bed, something like an electronic tablet. Viola, living alone, was likely a voracious reader, but what if it was something else?

"Dogs, stay!" she said, then climbed up onto the bed. Her knees sank so deeply in the pillowy mattress that crawling was awkward, but she managed to stretch and reach for the tablet without straying too far from the doorway where Girl watched intently, looking for any opening to rush in and seize the cat.

Scout sat cross-legged on the bed and looked over the tablet. It was a very old model, clearly designed for rough use, as it was heavy but durable. She found the on button and pressed it. She had a brief glimpse of a menu screen before an alert window popped open. No network connection. Given the state of the communications room, that wasn't exactly a surprise. She cleared the alert and went back to scrolling through the menu.

The tablet definitely wasn't designed for reading fiction. It must have belonged to the stationmaster originally, as the menu listed items for controlling payroll, expenses, inventory, travel logs, and other similar bits of bureaucracy.

Then Scout found the link to the station schematics. This was perhaps too much information, a screen full of overlapping colors designating plumbing, electrical conduits, emergency systems, and more things she couldn't even name. She summoned a submenu and began unchecking boxes until all she had left was an outline of the walls of the facility with little labels on each room.

There it was, off the hangar, just as she had suspected—and frustratingly close to the room she was sitting in, if she could just bust through walls. She reached out and touched the wall in front of her. Nope, far too solid. She was going to have to take the long way around.

"See you, Tubbins," she said, giving the cat's ears a scratch before clambering back out of the bed. She pushed Girl back with her knee before the dog could hop up on the bed and also give Tubbins's ears a go. "Come, dogs," she said, drawing Warrior's pistol and heading back through the red-lit rooms to the maintenance door to the hangar, tablet in hand.

There had been other doorways, once. The schematic showed doors on most of the walls of the octagonal rooms, but when Scout reached through the shelving to pass a hand over the walls, she felt no sign of a door. Over time, things had been sealed off, she guessed, although she couldn't imagine why. Viola said she had customers, but given the state of the hangar, they clearly weren't entering from there. Did everyone come through the long tunnel they had taken from the emergency beacon? But that required crawling on hands and knees through an all but invisible tunnel to the almost entirely blocked doorway. That didn't seem very customer-friendly.

And yet, the door was only *almost* entirely blocked. Did the wind really create that pattern, the emptiness within the hill? Scout doubted it. Someone had worked to keep that open, but only just. Now that Viola was gone, it hardly mattered. At some point after the storm, her customers would discover she was gone. And even if they were as standoffish and secretive as Viola, eventually the word would get out that all of this was just waiting here for the taking. Looters would follow.

Scout ducked through the maintenance door into the hangar, the dogs close at her heels. They were off-leash this time, but not anxious to run on ahead. Shadow sniffed at things as they passed them, but was careful to stay close to Scout's light. Girl padded along, uninterested in any of the mountains of junk around them.

As they drew nearer the utility room, Scout heard a soft clang, then someone whispering a curse. She gripped the pistol tightly, tucking Viola's tablet into the back of her belt to keep her other hand free. Shadow was sniffing the air like crazy, but Girl still seemed unconcerned.

They wormed their way around another stack of abandoned supplies, and Scout saw a faint light streaming from the doorway to the utility room. She kept her own light low on the ground just in front of her feet.

There was no disturbance in the thick layer of dust in front of her, only her prints and the dogs' behind her. That, plus Girl's continued calm, told her who she was sneaking up on.

She stepped into the utility room, pistol raised to just above hover chair height. "Hello, Liv."

23

LIV DIDN'T TURN AROUND. She had a panel from the wall removed and resting across the front of her hover chair as she leaned in to dig into the cables that had been behind it.

"I have a gun on you," Scout felt compelled to point out.

"Whatever makes you comfortable," Liv said, head still bent over her work. Scout looked at the pistol, then tucked it back away. Like Warrior had said, the most dangerous thing about Liv was her mouth. The gun would be useless against that.

"Why did you take out the power?" Scout asked.

"I didn't. I'm trying to turn everything back on," Liv said, reaching further into the cable-filled space.

"You can't just flip a switch?"

"Not anymore. Clementine left a nice collection of booby traps."

Scout watched her follow the length of a cable with her fingertips and pull out some sort of device that was attached to a number of other cables. She ran her hands delicately over it, trying not to disturb any of the junctions as she examined the cables.

"How do I know that's true?" Scout asked. "You could be booby-trapping it yourself just now."

"You don't know anything about these systems, do you?" Liv asked, carefully grasping a cable in one hand. She had a small tool in the other, either something that had been left in the utility room or something she had pulled from her chair. Scout wondered what else was inside that chair. It curved around Liv's folded legs like an egg. There was room enough for all manner of things. Perhaps even a weapon. And yet if Liv had a weapon, surely she would have brandished it before now.

"No, I don't," Scout admitted. "You can see why I can't exactly trust you when I don't know what it is you're doing."

"Scout, I'm tired. I don't want to fight you, physically or verbally," Liv said. Then she looked down at the dogs. "You trust your dogs, though, right? And your dogs don't seem upset with me at the moment." She stopped talking to focus on using the tool to detach the cable from the device. Only after she released a held breath did Scout realize that maybe Liv didn't know what she was doing either, not completely.

"I don't think my dogs are capable of recognizing the sort of threat you are," Scout said.

Liv laughed a surprisingly genuine-sounding laugh. "You're wise beyond your years, aren't you? Listen, just let me finish what I'm working on here and I'll explain all I can. We're not enemies. And with Clementine likely looking to take us both out, we might as well be allies."

"I might be better off on my own," Scout said.

"You might," Liv allowed. "But clearly I have skills you don't. And vice versa. That might be the only advantage we have."

Scout watched her work for a moment, then turned to shine her light back out in the hangar, as far as it could penetrate in every direction. There was no sign of Clementine. What was she waiting for? Why take out the lights and leave them exposed? She had left booby traps to slow them down, a distraction to tie them up while she accomplished something else.

"Do we really need lights that urgently?" Scout asked. "I don't like sitting still while she's on the move."

"Lights? Maybe, maybe not. Air? Well, even that might last us long enough, but I'd feel better with it running," Liv said.

"It is running," Scout said. "I felt it."

"It's cycling old air through the station, but it's not pulling in fresh air from the surface," Liv said, leaning forward once more to reach for more cables. "We're few, and the space is large. We could probably breathe just fine for the few days we still have to wait for the storm to pass, but I'd rather not rely on that. Especially if Clementine decides to get really creative."

"What do you think she'll do?"

"Seal us off if she can. Find more remote ways of killing us. She prefers to avoid confrontation, Warrior's death aside."

"And Ottilie's," Scout added, but Liv said nothing. "So you agree she's killing us off one by one."

Liv gave another little laugh, this one devoid of real humor. "I know she is. I know her well. Too well, maybe. Come here and hold this for me."

Scout moved closer but stopped just out of arm's reach. Liv held out an elaborate knot of cables in one hand, still fumbling in the wall with the other, and only looked up at Scout when she still hadn't taken what was offered.

"I'm not going to hurt you," Liv said.

"There could be live wires in there," Scout said.

"I assure you the power is still out," Liv said, but Scout refused to move. Liv sighed, taking her free hand out of the wall and leaning dangerously far out of her hover chair to extend it toward the dogs. Girl rushed eagerly forward to lick at her fingers. Shadow was more skittish, but in the end also touched his nose to the strange hand, then wagged his tail.

"That's not good enough for me," Scout said.

"If I don't fix this, we'll likely asphyxiate. Is that good enough for you?" Liv was getting testy.

"No," Scout said, lifting her chin. "I only have your word that we're even in danger here."

"Well, help or leave then."

"I'll do as I like."

"Stars save me from moody teens," Liv grumbled, balancing the knot of cables under one elbow so she could reach both hands inside the wall. She couldn't get in as far as she needed to and tried tucking the knot closer to her armpit. Still, she strained to reach whatever it was she needed.

Scout gave in with a sigh, gently extracting the knot of cables from under Liv's arm and holding it up as Liv traced the cables back into the wall.

A moment later, she sat back with another sigh of relief that made chills run up Scout's spine at the thought of whatever unknown danger they had just avoided.

"No lights," Scout said.

"Flip the switch," Liv said, waving a hand toward the other end of the room. Scout found the switch; being the master switch, it was quite obvious. As soon as she pushed it into the up position, the lights flickered back on and the tiny space was filled with the sound of wind. Scout looked up at a massive fan overhead, pulling in air from the surface. It must be nighttime out there; the wind on her face was briskly cold.

"You're going to explain now," Scout said, half shouting to be heard over the fan.

"Yes, but not here. And not in that hangar, either. Let's get back to the kitchen; I'm starving."

Scout wanted to argue, but Liv was already moving away, her hover chair floating noiselessly over the thick dust. The dogs trotted after her, Scout reluctantly bringing up the rear.

"Shouldn't we guard that?" Scout asked as she walked. "What's to stop her from just doing it again?"

"I put in a few traps of my own," Liv said. "Clementine may be clever, but not as clever as I am. I taught her everything she knows, not everything I know."

"Wait—taught her?" Scout repeated, but Liv nudged her hover chair up to a higher speed and she and the dogs had to jog to keep up.

The maintenance door was nearly too narrow for Liv to get her chair through. The widest part of the egg-shaped chair got jammed briefly, but she powered through. The metal of the doorframe scraped against the chrome side of the chair, shrieking in a way that made Scout's teeth hurt. She shone her light around the hangar behind them, worried the sound would draw Clementine out, but there was no sign of anyone.

She went through the doorway with the dogs and followed Liv back to the common room. Liv guided her chair around the pool of Viola's and Warrior's intermingled blood even though she wasn't about to come in contact with it, hovering as she was. A gesture of respect, perhaps, Scout thought.

"Is there anything to eat that isn't contaminated?" Liv asked, looking at the shattered remains of the biscuits and crackers strewn across the floor. Scout couldn't remember what had knocked the tray off the table, Viola's seizures or Clementine's kicking feet.

"MREs," Scout said. "I'll grab you a couple. Any preference?"

"Not at all," Liv said with another humorless laugh. "Never could tell one from the other, anyway."

Scout went into the pantry and gathered an assortment: two dinners for each of them, plus another two for the dogs. Then she grabbed a couple of bottles of jolo and went back out to the common room.

"Maybe we'd be safer in the kitchen?" she said. She wasn't sure if that was true, but she didn't savor the idea of sitting down to eat in a room cluttered with dead bodies, one of whom had been her friend, if only for a few days.

"If she's going to get us, she's going to get us. I'm done hiding," Liv said, but she guided her chair into the kitchen to park it at one end of the chopping block. Scout debated for a moment but then carried the food over to Liv without shutting the hatch. Being able to see felt like the safer bet.

Liv was holding out her hands for her share of the food. She took the two meals without comment but smirked as Scout handed her one of the bottles of jolo. "I haven't had this since I was a kid."

"Right now it's safer than the tea or coffee," Scout said, opening her own bottle. "I don't know how much has been poisoned or contaminated. Could be the leaves and beans, or the samovars, or the cups—"

"Or the water," Liv added, raising an eyebrow suggestively. She popped open her own bottle and took a long swallow. She grimaced. "I never liked it much as a kid. Always preferred the fizzy lemon drink. Do they still make that?"

"I don't know what that would be. Do you want me to look? Everything here is so old. I bet she has a few bottles," Scout offered.

"This will be fine for now," Liv said, activating the heating element on the first of her two meals. Scout handed her one of the titanium sporks she had found in the kitchen.

Scout opened two of the meals and served them to the dogs at room temperature. Then she warmed one of her meals, opened it up, and sporked some in her mouth without looking at the label. Liv wasn't wrong.

Girl paused in her eating, ears alert as she looked back towards the bathroom. Shadow looked up as well. Scout paused in her chewing, trying to hear what they were listening for. But they both went back to eating without so much as growling. Scout rose up from her chair, leaning over the table to look down towards the bathrooms.

"She's not coming. Not yet," Liv said.

"How can you be so sure?" Scout asked. "Because you 'know her'?"

"Yes," Liv said. She finished off her jolo in one long chug, then sat holding the bottle in her hands as if it were a fragile treasure. The sugar and caffeine that always made Scout's brain sing seemed to just make Liv melancholy. "She's going to come for me soon, but not just yet. And when she does, she will kill me."

"You say that like you have no intention of fighting her," Scout said.

"I don't. Aside from that just being generally useless, I'm done."

"Done fighting?"

"Done with living. But yes, that too."

"This wasn't your attitude a few hours ago," Scout said. "What changed?"

"Nothing. Everything. I don't know." She set the bottle aside and buried her face in her hands briefly. But she wasn't weeping, just waiting. At last she sat back, rubbed the back of one hand across her brow, and reached for her second meal. "I wasn't injured in the war, you know."

"No?" Scout said. She hadn't given it any thought one way or the other.

"No, I was paralyzed in an accident, when I was a kid. My parents had enrolled me in the exchange program. I was all set to go up into space, to train at working in free fall. Not everyone who went up there was allowed to stay, but I was prepared to work twice as hard. I wanted it so badly. But then the war broke out, and all of those programs were canceled."

"Ebba said after the war, the Space Farers took up all the wounded. Couldn't you have gone up then?"

"By then, it was already too late for me. I was tainted."

"Tainted?"

Liv took a deep breath. "I'm a spy. From the outbreak of the war. I was just seventeen. I had lost the opportunity of a lifetime and was quite despondent. Then a Space Farer approached me with an offer. If I enlisted early, got into communications, and passed key intel on to them, I would earn the right to live in space. Fool that I was, I leapt at the chance."

"You accused my parents of being spies," Scout said.

"I think they were. I don't know for sure; I never met another Planet Dweller spy or had direct knowledge of one, but I knew there were others working in secret alongside me. I'm certain there were. But if they're dead, it doesn't really matter anymore, does it?"

Scout said nothing. The melancholy, the regret dripping from Liv's every word was disturbing to her. Where was the cool manipulator now?

"I believed them. For a very long time, I believed them. But they kept putting off when I would get to go to space."

"The war ended years ago," Scout said.

"I know it. They promised me more—more space on the station and money and anything I could ever want. So I stayed and continued to spy. More than spy. There was little they didn't already know anymore, so to be valuable, to be worth everything they were offering me, I had to do more."

"You never saw anything they said they would give you? And yet you still believed them?"

"Once I turned over the first bit of intelligence, I had committed treason. Taking their further deals, a big part of that was because if I didn't, they'd have exposed me. I would be imprisoned."

"So you kept doing bad things against your own people?"

"I have no people," Liv said, practically spitting the words out. "Being a spy meant never getting close to anyone. I was barely older than you when I started."

"Did you give intel that led to the destruction of the cities?" Scout demanded.

"No, never," Liv said. "I swear. You saw how angry I was with Viola. I would be some kind of hypocrite if I accused her of my own crimes."

"Yes, you would be," Scout said.

"What I reported on was largely the movements of the governors. You might not remember, but during wartime, their locations were always secret."

"So the Space Farers wouldn't drop a rock on a city to take out a leader," Scout said. She remembered well.

"Rumors were always spread of secret tunnels under the cities, even of an underground train that took them from city to city. All lies. They were never in the cities at all. They stayed in places like this, or newer underground stations on islands just off the coast. Never in the cities."

"But if you passed that on to the Space Farers, then why did they drop asteroids on the cities? They knew their targets weren't there."

"Maybe to flush them out, to demoralize the Planet Dwellers, to destroy our economy. It was wartime; they made war."

"They were better at it than us," Scout said.

"The big guns hurt them. More than they let on," Liv said. "Which is why they decided not to risk another open war now."

"War isn't coming?"

"The Planet Dwellers are moving toward it, but the Space Farers see little to gain. If we hoard all the food, they suffer. But if they drop rocks on us until we submit, there's still no food and they still suffer. They have a different plan."

"You know their plan?" Scout asked.

"I implemented their plan," Liv said, the bitterness back in her voice. "Clementine."

"Clementine," Scout repeated. "She poisoned Ruth."

"Yes."

"But Warrior said that had taken place over a long time. Small doses building up, which was why the rest of us ate the same food as Ruth but were okay."

"Her target hadn't just been Ruth," Liv said.

"The governor. No hiding for him this time. You said you taught her?" Scout asked.

"Not everything. Killing, she already knew. I just finished off some of her technical skills. My primary function was teaching her to blend in here."

"Does she talk?"

"I've never heard her do so," Liv said. "I don't know why. My higher-ups never said."

"If her target was the governor, why did she leave with Ruth?"

"I don't know," Liv admitted. "I've tried a few times to pull her aside and ask, but she's giving me nothing. Clearly, she has a separate script from the one given to me."

"A separate script from the Space Farers? Or her own agenda?"

"I don't know," Liv said. "But there's one more thing I have to tell you."

"What?" Scout asked.

Liv jumped, clapping a hand to the side of her neck as if swatting a bug.

Scout lunged forward, pulling her hand away from her neck, but there was nothing to be seen but a tiny red dot. Had it been an insect? She looked into Liv's eyes and saw what was becoming an all too familiar sight: eyes desperate to communicate while a mouth moved soundlessly.

24

SCOUT JUMPED to her feet and ran to the doorway, the dogs charging after her, but there was nothing to be seen. No fleeing figure, no one lurking in the shadows. Had it really been an insect?

Just the thought made Scout's flesh crawl. Was this place really filled with killer insects too tiny to be seen?

Shadow barked his shrill warning cry and Scout turned back to see Liv pulling herself half out of the hover chair. Her body was starting to spasm, much as Viola's had, but there was a fierceness to her eyes. She likely knew what was happening to her, what poisons Clementine had access to, and their effects on the human body. She likely knew just how much time she had left, and despite her claim to be weary and ready to die, she was fighting for every last second of usable time.

She dumped the remains of her dinner on the chopping block and spread the tomato sauce smoothly across the surface. She dragged one shaking finger through the mess and Scout rushed to her side to see what she was writing.

NOT ALONE.

Liv flopped back into her chair, arms now nearly useless as the paralysis spread. Still, she managed to grope for something hidden inside her chair. She brought her hand back out, but the fist was clenched tight and Liv didn't seem to be able to force it to relax. Her eyes held Scout's, but if she was trying to impart some last meaning, Scout didn't know what it could be.

Then she was gone.

Scout looked at the words in the drying tomato sauce. They weren't alone. There was Clementine, but clearly that wasn't what Liv had struggled to convey to her.

Clementine wasn't alone.

Just how many child assassins trained in space was she trapped here with?

Scout looked at Liv's clenched hand. Was she going to have to break her fingers to find what she had? Would it even be worth it? Scout folded her hands over Liv's and found to her relief that she had relaxed in that last moment of life. The fingers parted easily and Scout felt two small disks fall into her palm.

She thrust them into a pocket, then reached into the chair to find the controls to send it out on its own into the common room with the other bodies. She made sure both dogs were with her, then she sealed the hatch.

They could shut off the power if they wanted to. Even the air. There would be enough in here to last her and the dogs a few more days.

Nothing was going to convince her she stood any sort of chance out there against an invisible stinging death.

Of course, she had no way of knowing those things weren't inside the kitchen with her even now, but if they were, there was nothing she could do about it.

Unless Warrior had something that could detect them?

Scout reached into the pouch for the scratched but otherwise intact lens that had covered Warrior's left eye. She brought it up to her face. It cut out the brightness of the overhead lights, but nothing more. Did it need body modifications to work? Like the power source or whatever in Warrior's back? She had been holding it a bit away from her face; she tried pressing it right up against her flesh.

It felt like it reached out for her and suctioned itself down over her eye, a startling sensation especially as it left her half blind. She fell back against the chopping block, fighting the urge to claw it back off her face.

Then it lit up, faint green lines outlining a space in front of her like a window. She waited for something more to happen, but that appeared to be it. She looked all around the room, hoping if there were any of the insects inside, the lens would detect them. Nothing happened. She didn't find that comforting.

Scout sat down on the floor, the two dogs once more snuggling in close to her. She found the belt pouch that contained the featureless tablet and set it on her left knee where her lensed left eye could easily focus on it.

There was a screen on it now, and a keyboard. Just like any other tablet. If she shut her right eye and only looked through the lens, it looked perfectly normal, not at all like the lens was superimposing an image on reality just for her. Weird.

The screen of the tablet had a message on it. She read DEAR GERTRUDE before looking away. That looked personal. Would Warrior want her seeing it? She had certainly never shared her name.

Scout set the tablet down and looked at the other gadgets one by one. Each had information superimposed by the lens, indicators or directions or, in the case of the gun, a number she guessed was the number of shots she had left to fire. Most of it was meaningless, except for the flare monitor. It had a feed coming from some place, perhaps from one of the Space Farer satellites, measuring current activity outside. As deep into the red zone as ever. A second screen showed the activity down where Scout was. A few particles were getting through even all the dirt and rock and station hull, but not much. Not enough to worry about.

After she had worked her way all around the belt, she took another jolo out of the fridge and popped it open. Then she dug the disks out of her pocket to examine them more closely. They both had the Planet Dweller government logo embossed on one side. They were the sort of disks one used to store data, Scout knew, but she had no device she could use to read them. She picked up Warrior's tablet again, but it had no input slots. She set it down and went back to turning the disks over and over between her fingers.

Government logo. Government property. Liv had been a spy; was this one last theft of intel destined for her Space Farer masters? But the disks were supposed to be able to hold massive amounts of data. Why would she need two?

Was one of them Ruth's? She had said she had intel with her that she had been taking to the rebels. Had it fallen into Liv's hands? Certainly no one else had gone looking for it in those chaotic hours after Ruth's death. When Scout had gone with Warrior and Ottilie to find Ebba, Liv had been left alone with Clementine, her protégé. She must have gotten it then.

Was there some point when Clementine had stopped working with Liv? It was all so confusing, trying to figure out who was on whose side. Scout put both of the disks back in her pocket and zipped it closed. She had all the intel now. That was all that mattered.

She took another drink of jolo. Her mind was both wired from the caffeine and exhausted, but she didn't dare sleep. If only she had searched Viola's medical supplies; she probably had something to keep a person awake that wasn't so teeth-grinding and heart-pounding as bottle after bottle of pure caffeine.

Scout rubbed at her forehead tiredly, felt the cold surface of the lens against the back of her hand and thought about taking it off again, but then reached for the tablet instead.

She carried Liv's secrets and Ruth's secrets, she might as well have Warrior's secrets too. Or Gertrude's.

Gertrude Bauer was a galactic marshal. That hadn't been a lie. Somewhere out there, closer to Galactic Central, she had a partner, Liam McGillicuddy. It looked like every time Warrior had been tapping away at this tablet, she had been corresponding with Liam.

Gertrude was technically on vacation. Her superiors knew she was dealing with a family matter and had given her an open-ended leave. But Liam knew she was really chasing down a fugitive, a low-level con artist too insignificant for the marshal service to bother with.

But he had made the mistake of ripping off Gertrude's grandma. Now Gertrude was going to make him pay.

She and Liam had a warm friendship, their messages back and forth full of references to things Scout didn't understand, like "that one time on Faver 4" or "just like Sonny Solu did back in the day." She guessed they had been friends a long time.

The last five messages were all from Liam.

THOSE HICKS GIVING YOU HELL, GERT?

UPDATE, GERT?

GERT, WHERE YOU AT?

GERT?

And finally: GERT, I KNOW YOU DON'T WANT ME TO BRING THIS TO SALVO'S ATTENTION, BUT COME ON. YOU CAN'T GO RADIO SILENT THIS LONG. GET BACK TO ME OR I'M SUMMONING THE POSSE.

Scout bit her lip. Should she answer? Pretend to be Gertrude and respond so he wouldn't panic? Tell him she was gone?

Ask him for help?

Scout touched the screen, opening a window for typing a response, but she still didn't know what to say.

The caffeine was making her dizzy, and her hands were shaking.

Warrior—Gertrude—had promised to take her off the planet. And Scout had seen that Liam already knew all about her. He knew Gertrude was planning to come back with a wide-eyed young thing in tow. Not how Scout would describe herself. Liam seemed convinced that Gertrude was joking. Not the sentimental type, his Gertrude. But if she spoke up, identified herself, explain what happened to Gertrude, would he see his friend's last wish through?

Scout rubbed at her forehead again. Something tasted weird in her mouth. The last bottle of jolo must have been a bit off. It was older than she was, she was sure.

Then she glanced down at the dogs, one on each side of her, both completely motionless. How long had they been like that? So still.

Too still.

Scout reached out a hand but immediately realized that something was very wrong. She felt more lightheaded than ever, and not in a too-much-caffeine/too-little-food kind of way.

Too late, she remembered what Viola had threatened. *You want me to vent all the oxygen out of that room?*

Shutting off the airflow wasn't the worst Clementine could do. She could actually pull all the oxygen out of the air. And Scout wouldn't notice until it was too late.

Scout pushed herself to her feet, vaguely hearing a crash as the tablet fell to the floor. Neither dog stirred, but she couldn't bother with them now. She stumbled/crawled to the hatch. It had to be just the kitchen Clementine was venting. If it wasn't, Scout was dead.

Scout's fingers fumbled at the bolt. She had just gotten it drawn back when everything went black. Lights out again?

A burst of pain at the back of her head told her that she had fallen. Then she knew no more.

25

SCOUT'S HEAD felt like it was full of sand, and the back of her neck was objecting to the extra weight pulling at it as her head dangled against her chest. Her wrists and ankles itched like mad.

Her hearing was fuzzy at first as she struggled to full wakefulness, but then her ears popped open as if she had just suddenly changed elevation. The murky underwater sounds in her ear were split by high-pitched voices chatting, one shrieking in giggles every few sentences. Scout rolled her head back and forced one eye open, then the other.

Warrior's lens was gone from her eye.

The lights were still on.

But she was far from alone.

Clementine was sitting cross-legged on top of the island in the kitchen, a slight smile to her lips as she looked down at the two other girls leaning against the counter and chatting up at her and with each other. They looked no older than Clementine. The taller of the two had short, spiky red hair. Not ginger, red like candy. She wore skintight shorts of bright pink and a loose-fitting short-sleeved shirt with such a riot of clashing colors Scout had to look away.

The other girl was smiling and talking as well, but her voice was gentle, almost pleasant. Her long black hair was neatly parted down the middle and plaited into two braids that extended past her shoulders, ending in demure white bows. She was wearing a pleated skirt and a round-collared blouse with a little black bow tie. She looked very clean, all save her white sneakers, which looked like she had competed in a hundred track-and-field events in them. They were worn familiarly around her feet, the leather scuffed and scarred, but the laces bright white and new.

"She's awake," the dark-haired girl said, noticing Scout gazing up at the three of them from beneath her brows. She couldn't quite bring her head up straight, not yet. Had they drugged her?

Clementine looked up at her and smiled.

The redhead turned to look as well. She might have been pretty if dressed and groomed more like the others. If the deep cut that curled up from under her chin to nearly the corner of her mouth hadn't left a scar. She walked up to stand an arm's length away from Scout, as if worried she was going to lunge at her. Scout tried to move her hands but then discovered the source of the itching sensation.

They had taken more of the cuffs from the pouch on Warrior's belt and tied her to one of the chairs. She had been unconscious, surely not struggling, but the cuffs were so tight her hands were turning blue. There was no way she could reach out to try to hurt this girl.

The girl seemed to know it. She grinned as Scout looked down at her own hands and then back up at the girl. She was standing there to make Scout aware of just how powerless she was.

"Clementine tells us you're Scout," the girl said. "I'm Beatrice, and that's Felicity. We're Clementine's oldest friends."

"She told you I'm Scout," Scout said. Her throat felt raw.

"In her own way, yes," Beatrice said, tipping her head to look at Scout from a different angle. Scout looked past her to Clementine, still perched on the counter. She could see the hilt of Warrior's pistol from where the girl had stuck it through her own belt. Warrior's belt was nowhere to be seen.

Neither were the dogs.

"My dogs," Scout said, rousting more fully awake. "Shadow, Girl. Where are they?"

Beatrice pulled a completely unconvincing look of sympathy. "I'm sorry. Venting the oxygen from this room was too much for them. I guess you're on your own now."

"I can take the blame for that," Felicity said. She was smearing peanut butter onto cracker rounds but raised a hand as if solemnly swearing she spoke true. "The bit with the oxygen was my idea. You *did* have the gun, you know."

"Where are they? Can I see them?"

Beatrice grinned and leaned in to speak directly into Scout's face. "They're right behind you. So no, I guess you can't."

Scout grasped the arms of the chair in her hands and started hopping madly up and down. The chair pivoted a bit, but not much. She saw Girl's black hindquarters, her white-tipped tail laying inert on the floor. Then Beatrice put her hands down on the arms of the chair, leaning her full weight in to stop Scout from moving.

Scout gasped. She should be able to shift a girl of this size, but she was incredibly heavy. Like Warrior had been.

"You have body modifications. All three of you?"

Beatrice laughed and turned her back on Scout to walk back to the others. Felicity shrugged as she licked peanut butter from her fingertips. Clementine just smiled.

"You can talk. And so can she," Scout said, pointing her chin at Felicity. "So why doesn't Clementine talk?"

"Who knows? She just never does," Beatrice said, facing Scout once more as she leaned back against the counter. She took one of Felicity's peanut butter–covered crackers and bit off half.

"Clementine hasn't spoken for as long as we've known her," Felicity said. "And we've known her longer than anyone."

"But don't judge her," Beatrice said. "She's the best of us. No one takes a mark out like Clementine."

"Well, she's also been training longer," Felicity said. "She got a head start."

"She'll always be the best," Beatrice said.

Clementine didn't seem to be paying attention to their compliments at all.

"Just how long has she been killing people?" Scout asked.

Beatrice looked up at Clementine. "How long, Clementine? Since you were five?" Clementine nodded. "Since she was five," Beatrice said to Scout.

"Murdering people at five? Sounds traumatic. Scarring. No wonder she doesn't speak," Scout said.

"Don't be so dramatic," Beatrice said, looking to Felicity. "I've been killing people since I was seven—"

"Seven as well," Felicity said with a nod.

"—and I don't have any scars. Not psychological ones, anyway," she added, touching the wound on her face.

"I wouldn't be so sure," Scout said under her breath.

"She's good at her job. Whether she can talk or not doesn't really bear into that," Beatrice said and reached for another cracker. "Liv told you all about Clementine, but she never mentioned us."

"Did she know about you?"

"Did she know about us," Beatrice scoffed, looking to Felicity, then to Clementine. "We grew up together, we three. We were smuggled down here together and into Liv's care. We didn't split up until Liv put us in separate houses for the assassin work. Yes, it's fair to say Liv knew us—what we were, what we did. I guess she wanted one last secret."

Scout lifted her buttocks off the chair. She shifted to a more comfortable position, but also she felt for the telltale lump of the two data disks in her pocket digging into her thigh as she moved. They were still safe, for now.

"Liv was afraid of us," Felicity said.

"Yes, right there at the end, she was. Felicity and I had both finished our assignments, but when we went to return home, Liv was gone. Disappeared. Even we with our sizable skills at finding people couldn't track her down. Not until Clementine just stumbled upon her all the way out here."

"And she called us," Felicity said. "And we came, because she's our sister."

"We've been helping ever since," Beatrice said. "Not with Ruth, of course, that was Clementine's particular task, but with the others."

"How?" Scout asked. "We searched everywhere and never saw any sign of you."

"We're very good," Felicity said.

Beatrice just pointed up at the ceiling.

Scout stared up past the light for some time before she saw what Beatrice was pointing at. The faintest of outlines. A hatch in the ceiling.

"Every room?" Scout asked.

Beatrice nodded. "Every room."

"No cameras up there," Scout said. "No motion sensors."

"Nothing," Beatrice agreed. "It's not easy to crawl about up there, true. It's cramped even for the likes of us. But we had full access to the whole compound and the rest of you never knew. Not even the marshal who thought she was so clever."

"We had a good laugh about her, didn't we?" Felicity said.

"Did we ever," Beatrice said.

"So now what?" Scout asked, heartsick. "Why didn't you just let me die with my dogs? Why did you open the door?"

"The air thing was my idea," Felicity said.

"Yeah, you mentioned," Scout said.

"Clementine didn't want you to die that way," Beatrice said. "She really likes you."

"I'm touched," Scout said from between gritted teeth.

"We do love her. She's our favorite sister, isn't she, Felicity?"

"She is indeed, Beatrice."

"So now what?" Scout asked again. "Are you going to cut me free? Give me a weapon? A fighting chance?"

Beatrice laughed long and loud, as if this was the funniest thing she'd heard in ages. "You think even with every weapon in this place and us with our bare hands, you would have a fighting chance?" Her laughter died as suddenly as it had started. "You wouldn't."

"So you're just going to kill me here in the chair?" Scout asked, tears of frustration making her vision swim. She twisted her hands in their bonds. The cuffs tightened, biting into her skin. Blood dripped to the floor. "Just do it then!"

Beatrice looked over at Felicity, who gave another bored shrug. They walked up to Scout, still squirming in the chair, step by deliberate step. Then they stopped an arm's length away, as if still worried she would somehow break free. Scout bit back a whimper of pain. She'd have to sacrifice a hand, and it still might not be enough.

"Rochambeau?" Felicity asked.

"Seriously?"

"Why should she be your kill?"

"Clementine says she wasn't yours."

"That's because she didn't like the oxygen deprivation thing. You got to kill the last one tied to a chair. I just got to poison the chubby one's tea. How is that any fun?"

"Oxygen deprivation isn't fun either."

"I *know*, that's why this one should be *mine*—"

Scout froze as Clementine appeared behind the two arguing girls, that smile of hers appearing over their overlapping shoulders like some demented sun. She raised her left hand, clutching Ottilie's little knife, and drove it straight into Beatrice's ear, promptly releasing it as Beatrice's knees buckled and she sprawled at Scout's feet. Then Clementine reached for Felicity, a hand gliding over her cheek as if she were about to draw her in for a kiss. Felicity seemed like she too wasn't sure if Clementine was about to kiss her or not, but when Clementine's hand tightened on the back of her neck and drew her in, the other hand sprawled across her face, twisting in the opposite direction.

Felicity made one last squeak of surprise. Then she too was sprawled at Scout's feet. Scout drew her toes back as far as she could, not wanting either of them or even one of Felicity's long braids to touch her.

Clementine stepped closer, bending to retrieve the knife from Beatrice's ear. Then she folded her arms, beaming down on Scout.

Scout had never been so terrified to have a friend.

26

"ARE you going to cut me free?" Scout asked, indicating the knife with her chin.

Clementine shook her head sadly.

"No witnesses?"

Clementine nodded.

"You want this to be a fair fight."

She shrugged one shoulder.

"But like your friend said, this can't ever be a fair fight. You have advantages I don't. So what is it?"

Clementine stepped closer, putting a hand on each arm of the chair and leaning in until her nose all but brushed Scout's. Her eyes stared into Scout's, demanding that she understand.

"I see," Scout said slowly. "You don't want a fair fight, but you do want a fight. Not death by poison or lack of air or invisible darts. You want me to fight with everything I have. Fight and fail."

Clementine grinned again, delighted that Scout understood her so well. Scout flinched as Clementine stepped back and tossed the knife into the air, but it came down gently onto Scout's lap.

Clementine brushed her fingertips over Scout's cheek as she ran past her. Then she was gone.

Scout looked at the knife on her lap. How long would Clementine wait for her to cut herself free before she came back to finish the job? She'd rather not find out.

It took more tries than Scout could count to get the knife balanced on her knees and then bring her knees up to where she could grasp the handle in her teeth. She had to give up on more than one attempt when the knife started to slide away from her; if it fell to the floor, she truly was lost.

She was exhausted in mind and body, bleeding profusely from each wrist and ankle, thickheaded still from the lack of oxygen not far enough in the past.

But she was still lucky. And once she had the knife in her teeth, cutting the bond from her wrist was surprisingly easy. Either that or her injured wrist was too numb to register pain as she sawed at the cord. After the first hand was free, the others quickly followed.

Clementine must have run back to the hangar, but Scout didn't follow. Instead, she fell to her knees beside her dogs, gathering Shadow up into her arms. He was cold already, and all the tears she hadn't shed since Warrior had died flooded out of her in a deluge. Clementine could come back and stab her from behind at any moment and she wouldn't know, wouldn't hear, wouldn't care. Shadow was all she had left of her family from before, and now he, too, was gone. She had nothing.

It wasn't a whimper, really, just a soft sort of complaining breath. Still hugging Shadow tight to her chest, she reached down to put a hand on Girl's chest. She was cold too, so very cold, but under Scout's palm, a heart was still sporadically beating.

"Girl," Scout said, giving the dog a shake, but she didn't wake. She tried again, louder and with more shaking, but still the dog slept on.

Perhaps there was something in the medical supplies to bring her out of it? Some sort of adrenaline?

Or perhaps she just needed to sleep it off?

Scout looked down at Shadow, still in her arms. She didn't want to leave him just lying on the floor, but she wasn't strong enough to lift both at once. She carried him first past the demolished communications room, through the barracks into Viola's rooms. She set him gently at the foot of the bed, pulling some of the comforters around him like a nest. He always liked to sleep under covers, even on the warmest of nights.

Scout went back and gathered the much heavier Girl up into her arms. Girl did whimper this time, but she still didn't wake. Scout brought her to the bed and put her inside a nest of covers as well. Viola's room felt warmer than the rest of the station. Perhaps the air was purer here as well. Perhaps it would be enough.

Tubbins lifted his head to look at Girl, but if he held any animosity toward the animal who had crushed his pelvis, he seemed to have let it go now that she too seemed in danger of death. Scout scratched his ears and listened to the loud rumble of his purr.

Then she went out to the hangar to find Clementine.

If she had been traveling through the ceilings before, she wasn't now. She had left a very clear path through the dust, even occasionally swiping a hand over a dusty tarp to leave a sloppy sort of arrow pointing the way.

She had the gun. Scout didn't know if she would use it, but she had it. Scout had Ottilie's knife as well as her own not-much-larger utility knife.

She also had her slingshot. Scout drew that out of her back pocket, taking a round stone from her side pocket and setting it in the cup. She kept it in her hands, not yet drawn back. It wasn't remotely as reassuring as a gun.

Then again, Scout had never seen that gun fire. She doubted it was defective, but she'd lay even odds that no one but Warrior could fire the thing. That seemed to be the way the bulk of her equipment functioned.

Did Clementine also have the lens? Could she fire with just one, like Scout had read the tablet with just one?

Scout bit her lip but kept following the trail of footprints. In the end, it didn't matter whether the answers were yes or no. Either way, she'd get maybe one good shot with her sling, and only if she was very, very lucky.

She wasn't surprised that Clementine had turned to watch for her approach, or that she was waiting for her under the open hatch Scout and Ottilie had found. Scout was certain now that this was how Beatrice and Felicity had entered. How they knew to come here, how Clementine had summoned them when she had never been left alone, would have to remain a mystery so long as Clementine remained silent.

Clementine had the gun in her hand, but was spinning it through her fingers, fast and nimble. Scout didn't waste what would likely be her only chance. She drew back and fired on Clementine, fishing out another stone before even looking up to see if she had hit.

Clementine's mouth was an almost comical gaping O as she wrung her hand and watched the spinning gun disappear into the darkness under a tumbling down stack of crates.

Scout drew back the next stone and fired. Clementine ducked, and the stone bounced off her shoulder. She straightened, her eyes dark with fury. She raised her hands, gesturing towards herself with her fingers. Scout didn't need a second invitation. She fired again and again. Clementine dodged the stones, never jumping for cover, preferring to simply twist her body out of the way each time. It was indescribably frustrating. Scout was a dead-eye shot with her sling, but that didn't matter, not against inhuman speed.

The last stone. Scout pulled it back and fired without aiming, screaming her rage as she sent the last of her hope hurtling toward the girl who was so much more than a girl.

Perhaps it was the scream, but Clementine hesitated. Not long—perhaps a fraction of a second—but long enough. The stone struck her square between the eyes and she stumbled back behind a pile of crates.

Scout took deep breath after deep breath, letting her anger go so she could focus. She didn't believe for a second that Clementine was down. She might be circling around her even now, keeping to the shadows that Scout's eyes couldn't penetrate or even crawling across the ceiling like a spider. Scout looked around and saw the gleam of metal in the dim light.

Someone had left a pry bar wedged between the slats of a crate, like they'd been in the middle of unpacking when they had just given up and walked away from all their belongings. Scout tucked the slingshot away and grasped the bar, putting a boot on the crate when she needed more leverage. At last, the bar pulled free, and she stumbled back.

She had a weapon. Unless Clementine found the gun, it was more than she had.

She started to raise it up as she walked closer to the light from the open hatch, but before she even had it halfway there, she was knocked to the ground. Clementine had circled around her—three-quarters of the way, at least—and the full weight of her knocking Scout to the ground was more than enough to drive every bit of air out of her body.

Scout wheezed painfully, unable to draw a full breath despite the stars in her vision. But she kept a tight hold on the pry bar.

Clementine climbed over her, one knee pressed tight to her side, the other coming down on the elbow of the arm with the pry bar. Scout whimpered as the bones in her elbow joint ground together. Clementine just smiled.

Her fingertips traced over Scout's face, brushing back the loose strands of sweat-dampened hair, then cupped her flushed cheeks. It was almost gentle, but Scout wasn't fooled. Not after what had happened to Felicity.

She heaved her entire body with all she had, but the girl was just too heavy. She couldn't budge her. Not even the hands softly touching her face were dislodged. They slipped past her cheeks, almost stroking her earlobes before positioning themselves on her neck.

This was it. She was going to tighten up now, and then Scout would be gone. It would all be over, as fast as switching off a light.

Scout closed her eyes. She wasn't afraid, not exactly, but she didn't want that lunatic grin to be the last thing she saw in this world.

A scream split the air. Scout thought at first that she was the one screaming, but biting her lip didn't cut off the sound.

She opened her eyes. Clementine was still straddling her, but now she was also showering her with blood. Or something like blood; even in the dim light, Scout could see the color was wrong.

Something in the darkness had a hold of Clementine's forearm. Scout saw bright white canines buried deeply in the flesh. Clementine screamed, sobbed, and struck at the thing. The thing pulled back, tearing a mouthful of Clementine's flesh away with it.

And exposing Clementine's shining metal interior.

The thing growled, then leapt again, this time striking higher and knocking Clementine off of Scout's chest. Scout raised the bar and brought it down hard on Clementine's blonde head. It clanged loudly and left a dent, but didn't stop Clementine's struggle with the darkness.

"Girl?" Scout said. Her eyes couldn't make sense of the whirl of motion in the half-light, but then the dog turned to look at her and she saw she was right. Girl had recovered, and had come to her rescue.

Clementine flung the dog off her and dragged herself with frightening speed across the floor. One arm hung useless against her chest, but the other was enough with her feet to propel her to the mountain of detritus under which the gun had disappeared.

"Girl!" Scout shouted, but too late. Clementine had the gun aimed at the dog. She rose slowly to her knees, then laboriously got to her feet without the use of either arm, her aim never wavering. Girl growled, every hair on her back standing on end in the most impressive threat display Scout had ever seen her do.

"Don't shoot her," Scout said, getting to her own feet with hands raised high. "Please. She's not a witness. Just me. It's not like she really hurt you. You have nanites too, right?"

Clementine never took her eyes off Girl. Her breath was coming in labored gasps, exertion and pain taking their toll. Scout was winded, too. She lowered her hands, then slipped one behind her to palm Ottilie's little knife.

She was only going to get one chance.

"Please, Clementine. It's just a dog."

For just a moment, the gun started to shake. Then it began to lower toward the ground.

But then she changed her mind, raising it again, finger starting to squeeze the trigger. Scout felt a rush of adrenaline, and for once she was the one moving with inhuman speed. She rushed to Clementine, seeing each motion as a separate frame of time. Step. Step. Grasp Clementine's arm. Not the shooting one, the wounded one. Use the arm to pivot around her body.

Bury the knife up to the hilt in the place where she was fairly certain the girl didn't have a kidney.

Clementine screamed again, then fell spasming to the floor. The gun went off and Girl yelped in alarm, but the shot was wild. In the distance, one of the mountains of junk underwent a minor avalanche of crates, tarps, and dust.

Then all was silent. Clementine was still. It was over.

Scout fell to her knees, then opened her arms for Girl to rush to her.

"Good dog," she said, sobbing into the dog's furry neck. She was wriggling, squirming excitement. A minute ago she'd been a hellhound intent on murder. Now she was just a puppy, albeit a badly trained one.

"Hey, Girl," Scout said. "You need a name. And I think I know just the one."

## 27

VIOLA'S BED was too soft, no doubt about it, but sometimes too soft could be quite nice. Now that she knew she was alone, she showered under the hottest water, washed every item of clothing, and hung them to dry from open locker doors, then crawled between Viola's covers and slept for what must have been more than a day.

It was divine.

She woke to the sound of Girl's bark, the cheerful yip-yip she did when she wanted Shadow to play with her. Scout felt her heart clench. All of that was gone now.

Girl yipped again, and Tubbins made a protesting meow. Scout sat straight up, anxious to prevent another mauling, but Girl wasn't even looking at the cat. Her butt was up in the air, her chin down on her forepaws as she bent forward to touch her nose to Shadow's, where Scout had left his body at the foot of the bed.

Scout blinked back tears, then leaned forward to brush Girl away. "Leave him be, now," she said. Surely the storm would end soon. Then she could bury her oldest friend beside her newest.

From within the nest of blankets came a sleepy, protesting growl of sound.

"Shadow?" Scout said, her hands shaking. She didn't have hope left in her heart. And yet... "Shadow?"

Shadow lifted his head to look at her. His body shook, his eyes looked strange, like he'd been drugged, but he was alive.

"Shadow!" Scout cried, fighting back the urge to scoop him up into her arms. He was clearly far too fragile for that. Instead, she moved closer to press her thigh close to his still colder-than-normal body. He lifted his head enough to rest it on her knee with a weary sigh, and she stroked his head as gently as she could. "Shadow, meet Gertrude," Scout said, reaching out with her other hand to scratch the ears of Gertrude, formerly Girl. Gertrude thumped her tail, nearly striking Tubbins, who meowed in annoyance but made no effort to move out of the way.

Scout went back to the showers to dress, then went to the kitchen. She no longer had the desire for any more jolo. Instead, she set Warrior's lens to her eye and found the device that detected poisons. She found the kettle uncontaminated and filled it with water and set it to boil, then located a clean mug and an unopened package of tea. Everything looked good through her lens. She reconstituted some freeze-dried eggs and even turned some of the stale bread from that fateful meal into slices of toast.

Once she'd eaten, she brought more beef stroganoff for the dogs. Shadow was moving a little, but it looked like his joints pained him. He ate some, mostly licking at the gravy, and didn't object when Gertrude turned to his tray when she was done with hers. Scout fetched a few bits of meat before Gertrude got to them and held them out for the cat to nibble at. He purred contentedly.

"Only a half a day left," Scout told them, consulting the readings on Warrior's device. "Then I guess we all roll out of here in Ebba and Ottilie's rover."

She reached into her pocket and took out the two data disks. Intelligence reports. The sorts of things that could change the course of a war.

If only she knew who to give them to.

There didn't seem to be good guys or bad guys. She would do

anything to prevent more rocks falling down on the cities, but she didn't know what that anything should be.

She kept turning those disks over and over in her hands, pausing only to fetch more food for her and the animals some hours later. What was she going to do?

At last she took out Warrior's tablet. There was another message on it. She had opened a reply window just before she had passed out from lack of oxygen. She had never typed anything, but she had apparently accidentally sent an empty message. Liam had replied. GERT, WHAT'S GOING ON?

Scout scratched at the skin around the lens on her face. She wasn't quite used to it being there. Not yet, anyway. She looked at the question again. WHAT'S GOING ON?

Then she answered it in great detail. In fact, with every detail she could recall. When at last she ran out of words, she touched the send command, turned off the tablet, and pulled the lens from her eye so she could wipe away the last tear she was going to let herself shed.

She had taken action. She was moving forward. No more clinging to the past.

Nothing was resolved, and yet she slept like a baby. In the morning she made more toast, eggs, and tea, then began searching Viola's station for anything worth taking with her on the rover. Food, medicine, clothing. There were far more things in those crates than Scout had use for, things like children's toys and decorative figurines from some time before planetfall.

At last, the flare detector beeped. The storm was over.

It took a few hours to load up the rover. Gertrude was beside herself, trying to both stay close to Scout and keep an eye on Shadow as he napped. She relaxed only when Scout lifted the little dog up into her arms and carried him back to the surface to nestle him into the nest she had made for him from Ebba and Ottilie's pillows. He sniffed all around himself but seemed to find their scents satisfactory and settled back down to resume his healing nap.

Scout left Gertrude to stand guard and went down to Viola's rooms one last time to scoop up Tubbins, pillow and all, and carry him up to the rover. Perhaps he'd be all right on his own in the station, living on vermin and whatnot, but somehow Scout didn't think that would be his happiest life. She had no interest in a cat herself, but someone in town would jump at the chance of taking him in. He was certainly a handsome enough cat, bright orange with white stripes like an alternate dimension's tiger, if a bit on the pudgy side.

Something on her belt beeped again and for a moment, Scout feared the storm had returned. But it was the tablet. Liam's reply was direct and to the point: MEET ME, followed by a date, time, and latitude and longitude. The tablet summoned up a map for her to see. He was directing her a little further out into the wilds, but not for three days yet.

Scout settled her father's hat more securely on her head and brushed red dust from the tunnel from the ragged remains of his shirt. Then she detonated the last of Ottilie's mining charges, effectively burying the remains of the nine others she had known only briefly but would never forget.

Then she hitched Warrior's belt a bit higher on her hips, touched her palm to the butt of the gun to make sure it was there, and pulled herself up into the rover.

Three days until Liam came for her. Time enough to find Tubbins a home.

Time enough to go back up into those hills and find herself a certain con artist.

# CHECK OUT BOOK TWO!

The Travels of Scout Shannon continue in Book Two, In Quaking Hills.

After spending the last four days of her life hiding out from a deadly solar particle storm in an underground bunker, trapped with six treacherous women and a trio of girl assassins, Scout Shannon just wants to find the man who conned her mentor and leave her home world for good.

Alas, the long-threatened war draws nearer and Scout finds herself caught in the middle, surrounded by rebels and bandits. Worse, she carries a pocketful of dangerous secrets with no one to entrust them to.

And the hills keep shaking. Something lurks deep underground. Something massive. Something world-destroying. Scout leaves in three days. If she lives that long.

"In Quaking Hills", the sequel to "Under Falling Skies" and the second book in "The Travels of Scout Shannon" series, a young adult science fiction novel for fans of plucky heroines, complicated boys, and loyal dog sidekicks.

In Quaking Hills, the second book in the Travels of Scout Shannon series. Check it out!

## NEW SERIES: THE FORGOTTEN PLANET

Coming soon from Ratatoskr Press Books, the new YA sci-fi series THE FORGOTTEN PLANET starts with book 1: Raiding the Forgotten Derelict.

**History sleeps beneath them all, but only she sees it.**

Lafayette Eloi always knew her parents thought differently from others. They kept their books buried beneath her mother's house. They spoke an old language in the dead of night, whispering behind closed doors and bolted shutters. She grew up in a village where no one was related to her, and she never knew why.

Then, after her mother died, her father came to fetch her. Now she and her mother's dog assist her father in his work. The work discussed in whispers in the dark. The work that had cost Lafayette so much all her young life.

But now she learns just how much her father's work means to their entire world. Only no one knows anything about it. Only her father. And only Lafayette.

Because the work that consumed her father's entire life and her mother's too now nibbles at the fringe's of Lafayette's own life. And she cannot refuse its call.

Raiding the Forgotten Derelict, first book in the new YA sci-fu series THE FORGOTTEN PLANET, available in September 2024 from Ratatoskr Press Books.

# COMPLETE SERIES: THE RITCHIE AND FITZ SCI-FI MURDER MYSTERIES

The Ritchie and Fitz Sci-Fi Murder Mysteries starts with Murder on the Intergalactic Railway.

For Murdina Ritchie, acceptance at the Oymyakon Foreign Service Academy means one last chance at her dream of becoming a diplomat for the Union of Free Worlds. For Shackleton Fitz IV, it represents his last chance not to fail out of military service entirely.

Strange that fate should throw them together now, among the last group of students admitted after the start of the semester. They had once shared the strongest of friendships. But that all ended a long time ago.

But when an insufferable but politically important woman turns up murdered, the two agree to put their differences aside and work together to solve the case.

Because the murderer might strike again. But more importantly, solving a murder would just have to impress the dour colonel who clearly thinks neither of them belong at his academy.

Murder on the Intergalactic Railway, the first book in the Ritchie and Fitz Sci-Fi Murder Mysteries.

# COMPLETE SERIES: THE TRAVELS OF SCOUT SHANNON

The complete six-book series THE TRAVELS OF SCOUT SHANNON begin with book one, Under Falling Skies.

Scout Shannon's whole family died the day the Space Farers dropped an asteroid on their domed city. Now she lives alone, out in the wild with only her dogs for company. She prefers it that way.

But Scout finds herself at a crossroads. One road leads back to a quiet life snug under the protective dome of a city. The other road leads to a life in the rebellion, a life of adventure and excitement but also danger. Dare she try to find the rebels hiding in the hills?

Then a chance encounter with a stranger from the other side of the galaxy threatens to derail what remains of Scout's life. The entire galaxy awaits her, if she survives the next four days.

"Under Falling Skies", a young adult science fiction novel, set on a remote planet with a distinctly Old West feel. For fans of gunslinging women and young girl assassins. And dogs.

Under Falling Skies, the first book in THE TRAVELS OF SCOUT SHANNON, available everywhere now.

# SCI-FI SERIAL PODCAST!

Check out my new monthly podcast of serialized science fiction: THE TALES OF THE CHAI MAKHANI TRIO!

Elyot loathes the massive Commonwealth ships that hover menacingly over his home world of Adghal. He hates the Commonwealth enforcers who harass the populace even more. But with his mother missing and presumed dead, Elyot keeps his head down and strives to avoid notice. And he succeeds until the day two strangers enter his life...

New episodes of this sci-fi serial drop every 1st of the month.

Now streaming on Apple Podcasts, Google Podcasts, Spotify, Stitcher and more. Also available in eBook and print everywhere books or sold. For a complete episode listing, check out the page on my website.

# ALSO FROM KATE MACLEOD

Love heists and capers? Then check out my new series, THE VIC HARPER CAPERS. The action starts with the novella THE THIRD POLE JOB.

Vic Harper and her gang retired wealthy from their life of thievery and heists. Whether in a luxury condo overlooking the river in Minneapolis or in a modernist mansion built into the side of a mountain in Colorado, life comes easy now.

Perhaps too easy.

When an old friend asks for a favor his niece, Vic and her mentor Chase Woodward leap at the chance to relieve a little of the boredom. But a quick bit of B&E in a wealthy suburb of Chicago leads to an even greater challenge.

The prize? Nothing much. Just the opportunity to level a playing field for their friend's niece.

But the heist? May prove to be their toughest ever. Because to get to the prize, they'll have to climb a mountain.

And not just any mountain. Their prize waits on the summit of Mount Everest.

THE THIRD POLE JOB, the first novella in the Vic Harper Caper series. For those who love capers, heists and other impossible missions.

Also from Ratatoskr Press, The Witches Three Cozy Mystery Series by Cate Martin, a mix of mystery and magic that begins with Book 1: Charm School.

Amanda Clarke thinks of herself as perfectly ordinary in every way. Just a small-town girl who serves breakfast all day in a little diner nestled next to the highway, nothing but dairy farms for miles around. She fits in there.

But then an old woman she never met dies, and Amanda was named in her will. Now Amanda packs a bag and heads to the big city, to Miss Zenobia Weekes' Charm School for Exceptional Young Ladies. And it's not in just any neighborhood. No, she finds herself on Summit Avenue in St. Paul, a street lined with gorgeous old houses, the former homes of lumber barons, railroad millionaires, even the writer F. Scott Fitzgerald. Why, Amanda can practically hear the jazz music still playing across the decades.

Scratch that. The music really, literally, still plays in the backyard of the charm school. Because the house stretches across time itself. Without a witch to protect this tear in the fabric of the world, anything can spill over. Like music.

Or like murder.

The complete series is out now, and it all starts with Charm School.

# FREE EBOOK!

Like exclusive, free content?

To get two prequel short stories to THE RITCHIE AND FITZ SCI-FI MURDER MYSTERIES as well as a bonus prequel novelette to the completed six-book series THE TRAVELS OF SCOUT SHANNON, signup for my monthly newsletter at KateMacLeodWrites.com.

Thank you!

# ABOUT THE AUTHOR

Photograph © 2016 Jonathan Conklin

Kate MacLeod has written stories which have appeared in Analog, Strange Horizons and Mythic Delirium, among other places. She is also the author of two young adult science fictions series: The Travels of Scout Shannon, and The Ritchie and Fitz Sci-Fi Murder Mysteries. She also contributes to a serialized science fiction podcast called The Tales of the Chai Makhani Trio. She currently lives in Minneapolis, Minnesota.

Find out more about the author and sign up for her newsletter at KateMacLeodWrites.com.

# ALSO BY KATE MACLEOD

**Novels**

**The Slums of the Solar System:**

Mitwa

The Mars of Malcontents

The Whole World for Each

Books 1-3 Box Set

**The Travels of Scout Shannon:**

Under Falling Skies

In Quaking Hills

Among Treacherous Stars

Against Impassable Barriers

Over Freezing Altitudes

At Galactic Central

The Travels of Scout Shannon Books 1-3

The Travels of Scout Shannon Books 4-6

The Travels of Scout Shannon Books 1-6

**The Ritchie and Fitz Sci-Fi Murder Mysteries:**

Murder on the Intergalactic Railway

Murder in the Skies

Body in the Catacombs

Death on the Summit

An Undiplomatic Murder

A Lethal Betrayal

**The Forgotten Planet**

Raiding the Forgotten Derelict (Forthcoming September 2024)

**Sci-Fi Novellas**

The Intergenerational Tree

I Rise into a Daybreak

**Caper Novellas**

The Third Pole Job

The Twelve Days of Christmas Job

**10-Story Collections**

Tales of Blood and Ink

Tales of Old Gods and New

**5-Story Collections**

Tales from Heian-Kyo and Others

Tales from the Edges and Ends

Tales from Forgotten Days

Tales from Ancient and Future Times

<u>Tales from Across Space</u>

www.ingramcontent.com/pod-product-compliance
Lightning Source LLC
Chambersburg PA
CBHW032000180726
48283CB00008B/2503